OLD MOORE'S

HOROSCOPE AND ASTRAL DIARY

LEO

OLD MOORE'S

HOROSCOPE AND ASTRAL DIARY

LEO

foulsham
LONDON • NEW YORK • TORONTO • SYDNEY

foulsham
The Old Barrel Store, Drayman's Lane, Marlow, Bucks SL7 2FF

Foulsham books can be found in all good bookshops and direct from www.foulsham.com

ISBN: 978-0-572-04495-4

Copyright © 2014 W. Foulsham & Co. Ltd

A CIP record for this book is available from the British Library

All rights reserved

The Copyright Act prohibits (subject to certain very limited exceptions) the making of copies of any copyright work or of a substantial part of such a work, including the making of copies by photocopying or similar process. Written permission to make a copy or copies must therefore normally be obtained from the publisher in advance. It is advisable also to consult the publisher if in any doubt as to the legality of any copying which is to be undertaken.

Typeset in Great Britain by Chris Brewer Origination, Christchurch

CONTENTS

1	Introduction	6
2	The Essence of Leo: Exploring the Personality of Leo the Lion	7
3	Leo on the Cusp	13
4	Leo and its Ascendants	16
5	The Moon and the Part it Plays in your Life	24
6	Moon Signs	28
7	Leo in Love	32
8	Venus: The Planet of Love	36
9	Venus through the Zodiac Signs	38
10	The Astral Diary: How the Diagrams Work	42
11	Leo: Your Year in Brief	44
12	Leo 2015: Diary Pages	45
13	How to Calculate Your Rising Sign	124
14	Rising Signs for Leo	125
15	The Zodiac, Planets and Correspondences	127

INTRODUCTION

Astrology has been a part of life for centuries now, and no matter how technological our lives become, it seems that it never diminishes in popularity. For thousands of years people have been gazing up at the star-clad heavens and seeing their own activities and proclivities reflected in the movement of those little points of light. Across centuries countless hours have been spent studying the way our natures, activities and decisions seem to be paralleled by their predictable movements. Old Moore, a time-served veteran in astrological research, continues to monitor the zodiac and has produced the Astral Diary for 2015, tailor-made to your own astrological makeup.

Old Moore's Astral Diary is unique in its ability to get the heart of your nature and to offer you the sort of advice that might come from a trusted friend. It enables you to see in a day-by-day sense exactly how the planets are working for you. The diary section advises how you can get the best from upcoming situations and allows you to plan ahead successfully. There's also room on each daily entry to record your own observations or appointments.

While other popular astrology books merely deal with your astrological 'Sun sign', the Astral Diaries go much further. Every person on the planet is unique and Old Moore allows you to access your individuality in a number of ways. The front section gives you the chance to work out the placement of the Moon at the time of your birth and to see how its position has set an important seal on your overall nature. Perhaps most important of all, you can use the Astral Diary to discover your Rising Sign. This is the zodiac sign that was appearing over the Eastern horizon at the time of your birth and is just as important to you as an individual as is your Sun sign.

It is the synthesis of many different astrological possibilities that makes you what you are and with the Astral Diaries you can learn so much. How do you react to love and romance? Through the unique Venus tables and the readings that follow them, you can learn where the planet Venus was at the time of your birth. It is even possible to register when little Mercury is 'retrograde', which means that it appears to be moving backwards in space when viewed from the Earth. Mercury rules communication, so be prepared to deal with a few setbacks in this area when you see the sign ☿. The Astral Diary will be an interest and a support throughout the whole year ahead.

Old Moore extends his customary greeting to all people of the Earth and offers his age-old wishes for a happy and prosperous period ahead.

THE ESSENCE OF LEO

Exploring the Personality of Leo the Lion

(23RD JULY – 23RD AUGUST)

What's in a sign?

What really sets you apart from the herd is your naturally cheerful tendencies and your ability to display a noble and very brave face to the world at large. Leos are big people, no matter what their physical size may be and it is clear that you could never be an 'also-ran'. Quite the reverse is usually the case because you are at the forefront of many ventures, ideas and enterprises.

Being a Leo brings quite a few responsibilities. For example, people tend to look up to you, which means you have to be on your best behaviour for a lot of the time. Not that this prevents you from showing a slightly mischievous face to the world on a regular basis. You are not given to worrying too much because you generally know how to get yourself out of any sort of difficulty with ease. It's true that you tend to face problems head-on – a natural extension of your rather courageous temperament. Sometimes this can get you into unnecessary scrapes, as can your tendency to pit yourself against the forces of nature, or social groups that you feel to be absolutely wrong in their intentions or objectives.

As a Leo you do recognise that you have a responsibility to others, particularly those types who are shyer than you, or individuals who just don't have the ability to look after themselves. With a smile and a shrug you are inclined to put a protecting arm around the whole world. In effect you are the perfect big brother or sister and take pride in the position you tend to gain in society. In a work sense you are capable and can very easily find yourself in a situation of responsibility. You don't worry about this and can make a fine executive in almost any profession. There's no doubt though that you are naturally best placed at the head of things.

The Essence of Leo

It's true that you are inclined to do too much and that your levels of energy are far from inexhaustible. However, it's a love of life that counts for the most in your case, and nothing is going to prevent you from being the happy, sunny, freewheeling soul that represents the sign of Leo at its very best.

Leo resources

Your ruling planet is the Sun, the source of all heat, light and therefore life on the Earth. The Sun is fundamental to our very existence, and its primary importance at the centre of things is reflected in your nature. Unlike your brother sign, Aries, you display your Fire-sign tendencies in a more controlled manner and without the need to dominate to such a great extent. All the same your natural position is at the head of things and this is reflected in the resources you draw from the zodiac.

One of your greatest gifts is a natural tendency to look confident, even on those occasions when you might be quaking inside. It's amazing what a difference this makes because it more or less ensures that others will trust you and tend to follow your lead. Once they do you rise to the occasion in an admirable way because you don't want to let your followers down. In almost any situation that life could present, you will quite naturally take charge, and those around you are invariably happy that it should be so.

Most Leos are capable in a practical as well as a theoretical way but a hands-on approach probably works best. Leo leads from the front, which means having to keep fit and healthy. This is vital, but like the lion that your sign represents you can get rather lethargic and flabby if you don't keep in shape. Also like the lion you do have a tendency to appear lazy on occasions, but only usually when things are already running smoothly around you.

The professions chosen by Leos are many and varied. It isn't really the subject matter that is important, merely your ability to make an impression. At work, as well as in social situations, you can shine like the very Sun that rules you. Usually well liked and respected, you are in a position to utilise the popularity that comes your way in order to feather your own nest, as well as those of people around you. Domestically speaking you have a great love of home and family, though you might tend to stifle those you love a little on occasions.

Beneath the surface

'What really makes me tick?' A fair question, and one that members of many zodiac signs are constantly inclined to ask themselves – but not you. The fact is that you are not the deepest thinker around. This is not to suggest that you don't have lofty ideals or a very sound moral base to your behaviour. The reason that you probably are not one of life's natural philosophers is because you are a 'doer'. In the time it takes others to mull over any given situation you will have sorted it out and moved on to the next task. However, this is a natural skill that can be honed to perfection and depends in part on getting yourself interested in the first place.

Your boredom threshold tends to be quite low and you would soon feel fatigued if you were forced to remain in situations which meant doing the same thing time and time again. Your driving, sometimes impatient mentality does demand change, and you can become irritable and out of sorts if you don't find it.

Are you as confident as you often appear to be? The answer to that one has to be yes. The fact is that you quite often fail to bear in mind the possibility of failure. Of course this means that you are more disappointed than most when things do go wrong, but your very conviction often leads to success. Once you do get down in the dumps however, you can be a very sorry picture indeed. Fortunately, you have the mental and spiritual reserves to pick yourself up fairly quickly and to push forward once again.

In matters of love you are probably more reserved than you give the impression of being. All the same you know how to deal with relationships – that is until you start acting like a lion again. The over-protective quality of your animal sign is always a danger, and one that you need to control. Perhaps here we find the Achilles heel of Leo. It is quite common for you to experience a sense of jealousy, a fact that would make you more possessive than usual. You have to remember that it's fine to love, but impossible to 'own' another individual.

In the main you offer the world an exterior smile that reflects your genuine inner state. Truthfulness shows on your face, and is usually felt in your heart in equal proportion.

The Essence of Leo

Making the best of yourself

To feel good and to make the right sort of impression, you have to look good too. Nobody goes to the safari park to see a moth-eaten lion. You can dress cheaply, but you have to cut a dash in some way. Drab colours definitely don't suit your personality, with bright oranges and yellows being the most favoured – a reflection of your Sun rulership. Once you are properly attired you tend to move forward positively through life. Most Leos are quite attractive people, mainly because the honesty, frankness and genuine courage of your personality has a habit of finding its way to the surface.

There is one line of Kipling's famous poem 'If' that springs to mind as an object lesson for Leo, this being 'And yet don't look too good, nor talk too wise'. It is quite possible for you to go over the top in your enthusiasm and even courage isn't same thing as foolhardiness. A little humility can go a long way, as can a determination to learn from people who know better than you do. Constantly knocking your head against the same brick wall isn't very productive, and can sometimes be avoided by simply showing a willingness to take advice. And it isn't as if people are unwilling to lend a hand. The Leo subjects who achieve the most in life have learned how to co-operate, though without feeling that they are having to relinquish the leading position in life that is so important to them.

In order for you truly to make the best of yourself you also need to be fit. Leos are inclined to have some problems associated with the heart and the circulatory system, so you need to exercise regularly and to avoid the sort of constant stress that can lead to longer-term health difficulties. To most Leos laughter is the best tonic of all.

The impressions you give

If we could all genuinely see ourselves as others see us, how much easier would be our interaction with the world at large? Yours may not be the most intuitive sign of the zodiac but you are perceptive enough to know when you are giving the right impression. If this fact is sometimes obscured it is at least easy for you to monitor when things are not going right. In turn this should result in a slight modification of your own personality to take account of circumstances.

If you have any specific problem in this direction it stems from the fact that you are not a natural philosopher. Doing is far more important than thinking to you, a truism that can sometimes be your downfall. More attention to detail and a better appraisal of others allow you to offer a much better impression of yourself.

Most people already find you sunny, warm, frank, free, delightfully outspoken and very brave. All you have to do to achieve real success is to build on the qualities you already possess and to make allowance for the fact that the world is full of individuals. You can't browbeat others into liking you, even though popularity is important to you. There will always be people who don't take to your personality and there really isn't much you can do about the situation.

A great advantage for you is that it isn't difficult for you to appear to know what you are talking about, even when you don't. You can gain extra skills on the way and should use the very real magnetism of your personality both to help the world and to improve your own situation. Few people would find you easy either to dismiss or to forget, which can be another very definite advantage in life.

A sense of proportion is sometimes important, as well as a defined purpose in your statements and actions. All in all you have most of the components that allow you to be popular. Build on these and your true Leo worth will be there for all to see.

The Essence of Leo

The way forward

No sign of the zodiac typifies its planetary ruler more than your own sign of Leo. When you smile, the Sun comes out and your laughter is so infectious that even the hardest-hearted types would be likely to smile themselves. Add to this the fact that you typify the statement 'fools rush in where angels fear to tread' and you have a formidable combination at your disposal. It might be the case that you fail to take account of some of your actions, but a good-humoured and intelligent attitude to life also allows you to get out of scrapes as easily as you get into them.

Cultivate your tendency to stick up for the underdog and don't get yourself into a position in life that means you constantly have to pay lip service to people who clearly don't know what they are doing. You can't stand incompetence, arrogance, cruelty or oppression. Of course this is a fine attitude, but you can't put the world right on your own, so once again co-operation proves to be the key to success.

In a career sense you need to be doing something that constantly stretches you. Your boredom threshold is not high and with constant tedium can come a worrisome streak and a tendency to health difficulties. Variety in work is the spice of your life, together with an active and useful social life, which is also vitally important.

In matters of love you are sincere and ardent, though with a tendency towards being a little too possessive. Allowing others the freedom to go their own way means finding more happiness yourself and lifts the noble qualities of your nature to new heights. Leos are still more likely than people from other zodiac signs to find one important relationship in life and to stick with it. Part of the reason for this state of affairs is that you have a horror of failure and will persist, even when others fall by the wayside.

You may not be creative in the generally accepted sense of the word but you have a good eye for colour and enjoy cheerful surroundings. Practical and capable, you won't need to call on the services of experts too often, since Leos generally don't shy away from DIY chores.

Diet is vitally important because as a Leo you are inclined to put on weight readily. Exercise helps here and is something you revel in anyway. Use your natural talents to the full, defend the weak and fight oppressors and you can't go far wrong in your life. Most important of all, keep smiling. You are tremendous fun to have around.

LEO ON THE CUSP

Old Moore is often asked how astrological profiles are altered for those people born at either the beginning or the end of a zodiac sign, or, more properly, on the cusps of a sign. In the case of Leo this would be on the 23rd of July and for two or three days after, and similarly at the end of the sign, probably from the 21st to the 23rd of August. In this year's Astral Diaries, once again, Old Moore sets out to explain the differences regarding cuspid signs.

The Cancer Cusp – July 23rd to July 25th

You tend to take life at a slower pace than Leo when taken on its own. You are more sensitive and quieter by nature, with slightly less drive and enthusiasm and a less dynamic disposition. With a creative and generally aspiring nature, you draw from Leo the fearless qualities that are typical of the sign, but these only tend to show on those occasions when you feel very strongly about things. There is quite a contradiction between these two signs and therefore you have a tendency to show very different faces in different circumstances. This fact makes you slightly awkward to predict and you often shock people as a result. Just when the world thinks it has you pigeon-holed, off you go at a tangent, perplexing your relatives and friends all over again. Family members are very important to you and when your aspiring and lofty qualities show most it is often on their behalf. In matters of love you tend to be very loyal, and have the ability to mix very well with others, enjoying cheerful and original people as part of your social circle.

One area that needs particular attention is your health. Although generally more robust than you probably give yourself credit for, you get through a tremendous amount of nervous energy, much more than others may realise. You need to watch your diet very carefully and to avoid acidic foods, which can upset your stomach. Apart from this, however, you are virtually indestructible and have the capacity to work long and hard to achieve your objectives.

At work you do your best to be adaptable and are very good at managing others. The natural frustrations of Leo, when faced with opposition, are less accented in your case. You have the ability to get on well and should make a mark for yourself when happy with your lot. Few would find you overbearing or bossy, although at times you seem to lack some of the natural Leo confidence. Most important of all though – you are kind, generous, trusting and very good to know.

The Virgo Cusp – August 21st to August 23rd

Perhaps the greatest difficulty for people born under the influence of this cusp is in making themselves understood. You probably think that you are the least complicated person in the world, but that isn't the way others see you. Your nature is full of contradictions. On the one hand you are fanatically tidy, and yet you can work in a state of almost total chaos; you love to travel and yet, deep inside, you are a home bird; and you talk a great deal, but often with quiet confidence. To disentangle all these contradictions is as difficult for you as it is for anyone else, and so you may often not reach the level of self-confidence that you deserve.

You have most of the positive qualities associated with the zodiac sign of Leo and your lofty, aspiring, sunny disposition is usually well accepted. Beneath this, however, is a quiet and contemplative person, who needs moments alone to synthesise the many happenings in a busy life. Usually physically robust, you do tend to worry more than is good for you, frequently about matters that are not particularly important. Meditation suits you well, particularly the kind that has a physical aspect, as this satisfies your Leo qualities, too. With a nervous system that varies from day to day, it is important for you to be sure that you achieve the level of relaxation that is vital to your Virgoan qualities. For you this could be anything between a crossword puzzle and two weeks on a cruise ship. In social settings you enjoy a degree of variety and can manage quite well with new people, even though you often tend to stick to people with whom you are familiar.

Leo on the Cusp

It's always important for you to keep an open mind and you shouldn't allow negative thoughts to build up. Keeping busy makes sense, as long as you don't continually choose to burn the candle at both ends. The people who know you the best do find you difficult to understand, but they are inclined to love you all the more for that. The most important character trait for you to cultivate is optimism because the more cheerful you remain regarding the future, the greater is the effort you expound upon it.

LEO AND ITS ASCENDANTS

The nature of every individual on the planet is composed of the rich variety of zodiac signs and planetary positions that were present at the time of their birth. Your Sun sign, which in your case is Leo, is one of the many factors when it comes to assessing the unique person you are. Probably the most important consideration, other than your Sun sign, is to establish the zodiac sign that was rising over the eastern horizon at the time that you were born. This is your Ascending or Rising sign. Most popular astrology fails to take account of the Ascendant, and yet its importance remains with you from the very moment of your birth, through every day of your life. The Ascendant is evident in the way you approach the world, and so, when meeting a person for the first time, it is this astrological influence that you are most likely to notice first. Our Ascending sign essentially represents what we appear to be, while the Sun sign is what we feel inside ourselves.

The Ascendant also has the potential for modifying our overall nature. For example, if you were born at a time of day when Leo was passing over the eastern horizon (this would be around the time of dawn) then you would be classed as a double Leo. As such, you would typify this zodiac sign, both internally and in your dealings with others. However, if your Ascendant sign turned out to be a Water sign, such as Pisces, there would be a profound alteration of nature, away from the expected qualities of Leo.

One of the reasons why popular astrology often ignores the Ascendant is that it has always been rather difficult to establish. Old Moore has found a way to make this possible by devising an easy-to-use table, which you will find on page 125 of this book. Using this, you can establish your Ascendant sign at a glance. You will need to know your rough time of birth, then it is simply a case of following the instructions.

For those readers who have no idea of their time of birth it might be worth allowing a good friend, or perhaps your partner, to read through the section that follows this introduction. Someone who deals with you on a regular basis may easily discover your Ascending sign, even though you could have some difficulty establishing it for yourself. A good understanding of this component of your nature is essential if you want to be aware of that 'other person' who is responsible for the way you make contact with the world at large. Your Sun sign, Ascendant sign, and the other pointers in this book will, together, allow you a far better understanding of what makes you tick as an individual. Peeling back the different layers of your astrological make-up can be an enlightening experience, and the Ascendant may represent one of the most important layers of all.

Leo with Leo Ascendant

This is a combination that could make even Old Moore breathless! The fact is that you are a go-getter of the first order, and there is virtually nothing in life that would prevent you from getting what you want. The problem here is that once you have it, you probably want something else. All in all you could end up like a dog chasing its own tail and so the first advice is to slow down and enjoy the journey a little more. Not that all of this makes you any less likeable, or indispensable, to a whole host of people. You smile much more often than you scowl and you won't make heavy weather of problems that would rock others back on their heels.

You are rather materialistic, and ultimate success probably means more to you than it should, but you can easily stop on your hectic journey to take note of those who have fallen by the wayside and give them a helping hand. If all that power is used for the good of humanity you might even become a living saint, except for the fact that you would be too busy to accept the honour. Be careful that you don't weigh yourself down with so many responsibilities that you fail to notice your progress, and travel as much as you can because this will certainly broaden your mind. Most people find you very attractive and fun to have around.

Leo with Virgo Ascendant

Here we have cheerfulness allied to efficiency, which can be a very positive combination for most of the time. With all the sense of honour, justice and bravery of the Leo subject, Virgo adds better staying power through tedious situations and offers you a slightly more serious view of life than we would expect from the Lion alone. In almost any situation you can keep going until you get to your chosen destination and you also find the time to reach out to the people who need your unique nature the most. Few would deny your kindness, though you can attract a little envy because it seems as though yours is the sort of personality that everyone else wants.

Most people born with this combination have a radiant smile and will do their utmost to think situations through carefully. If there is any tendency to be foolhardy, it is carefully masked beneath a covering of Virgoan common sense. Family matters are dealt with efficiently and with great love. Some might see you as close one moment and distant the next. The truth is that you are always on the go and have a thousand different things to think about, all at the same time. On the whole your presence is noticed, and you may represent the most loyal friend of them all.

Leo with Libra Ascendant

Libra brings slightly more flexibility to the fixed quality of the Leo nature. On the whole you do not represent a picture that is so very different from other versions of the Lion, though you find more time to smile, enjoy changing your mind a great deal more and have a greater number of casual friends. Few would find you proud or haughty and you retain the common touch that can be so important when it comes to getting on in life generally. At work you like to do something that brings variety, and would probably soon tire of doing the same task over and over again. Many of you are teachers, for you have patience, allied to a stubborn core. This can be an indispensable combination on occasions and is part of the reason for the material success that many folk with this combination achieve.

It isn't often that you get down in the dumps, as there is generally something more important around the next corner and you love the cut and thrust of everyday life. You always manage to stay young at heart, no matter what your age might be, and you revel in the company of interesting and stimulating types. Maybe you should try harder to concentrate on one thing at once and also strive to retain a serious opinion for more than ten minutes at a time, although Leo does help to control any flighty tendencies which show up.

Leo with Scorpio Ascendant

A Leo with intensity, that is what you are. You are committed to good causes and would argue the hind leg off a donkey in defence of your many ideals. If you are not out there saving the planet you could just be at home in the bath, thinking up the next way to save humanity from its own worst excesses. In your own life, although you love little luxuries, you are sparing and frugal, yet generous as can be to those you take to. It's a fact that you don't like everyone and of course the same is true in reverse. It might be easier for you to understand why you dislike others than to appreciate the reverse side of the coin, for your pride can be badly dented on occasions. Scorpio brings a tendency to have down spells, though the fact that Leo is also strongly represented in your nature should prevent them from becoming a regular part of your life.

It is important for you to learn how to forgive and forget, and there isn't much point in bearing a grudge because you are basically too noble to do so. If something goes wrong, kiss the situation goodbye and get on with the next interesting adventure, of which there are many in your life. Stop-start situations sometimes get in the way but there are plenty of people around who would be only too willing to lend a helping hand.

Leo with Sagittarius Ascendant

Above and beyond anything else you are naturally funny, and this is an aspect of your nature that will bring you intact through a whole series of problems that you manage to create for yourself. Chatty, witty, charming, kind and loving, you personify the best qualities of both these signs, whilst also retaining the Fire-sign ability to keep going, long after the rest of the party has gone home to bed. Being great fun to have around, you attract friends in the way that a magnet attracts iron filings. Many of these will be casual connections but there will always be a nucleus of deep, abiding attachments that may stay around you for most of your life.

You don't often suffer from fatigue, but on those occasions when you do there is ample reason to stay still for a while and simply take stock of situations. Routines are not your thing and you like to fill your life with variety. It's important to do certain things right, however, and staying power is something that comes with age, assisted by the fixed quality of Leo. Few would lock horns with you in an argument, which you always have to win. In a way you are a natural debator but you can sometimes carry things too far if you are up against a worthy opponent. Confidence is not lacking and you go with ease through situations that would cause many people to give up.

Leo with Capricorn Ascendant

What really sets you apart is your endless patience and determination to get where you want to go, no matter how long it takes you to do so. On the way there are many sub-plots in your life and a wealth of entertaining situations to keep you amused. Probably somewhat quieter than the average Leo, you still have the capacity to be the life and soul of the party on those occasions when it suits you to be so. Energy, when allied to persistence, is a powerful commodity and you have a great need to take on causes of one sort or another. Probably at your best when defending the rights of the oppressed, you take the protecting qualities of Leo to greater heights than almost anyone else who is touched by the idealistic and regal qualities of the sign. If arguments come into your life, you deal with them quickly and, in the main, wisely. Like most Capricorn types, you take to a few individuals who will play a part in your life for years on end.

Being a good family type, your partner and children are extremely important and you will lavish the same patience, determination and ultimate success on their behalf that you do when dealing with more remote situations. The fact is that you do not know any other way to behave and you are at your best when there is some mountain to climb.

Leo with Aquarius Ascendant

All associations with Aquarius bring originality, and you are no exception. You aspire to do your best most of the time, but manage to achieve your objectives in an infinitely amusing and entertaining way. Not that you set out to do so, because if you are an actor on the stage of life, it seems as though you are a natural one. There is nothing remotely pretentious about your breezy personality or your ability to occupy the centre of any stage. This analogy is quite appropriate because you probably like the theatre. Being in any situation when reality is suspended for a while suits you down to the ground, and in any case you may regularly ask yourself if you even recognise what reality is. Always asking questions, both of yourself and of the world at large, you soldier on relentlessly, though not to the exclusion of having a good time on the way.

Keeping to tried and tested paths is not your way. You are a natural trail-blazer who is full of good ideas and who has the energy to put them into practice. You care deeply for the people who play an important part in your life, but are wise enough to allow them the space they need in order to develop their own personalities along the way. Most people like you, many love you, and one or two think that you are the best thing since sliced bread.

Leo with Pisces Ascendant

You are a very sensitive soul, on occasions too much so for your own good. However, there is no better advocate for the rights of humanity than you, and you constantly do what you can to support the downtrodden and oppressed. Good causes are your thing and there are likely to be many in your life. You will probably find yourself pushed to the front of almost any enterprise of which you are a part because, despite the deeper qualities of Pisces, you are a natural leader. Even on those occasions when it feels as though you lack confidence, you manage to muddle through somehow, and your smile is as broad as the day. Few sign combinations are more loved than this one, mainly because you do not have a malicious bone in your body and will readily forgive and forget, which the Lion on its own often will not.

Although you are capable of acting on impulse, you do so from a deep sense of moral conviction, so that most of your endeavours are designed to suit other people too. They recognise this fact, and will push a great deal of support back in your direction. Even when you come across troubles in your life you manage to find ways to sort them out, and will invariably find something new to smile about on the way. Your sensitivity rating is massive and you can easily be moved to tears.

Leo with Aries Ascendant

Here we come upon a situation in which Leo is allied with another Fire sign. This creates a character that could appear to be typically Aries at first sight and in many ways it is, though there are subtle differences that should not be ignored. Although you have the standard Aries ability for getting things done, many of the tasks you do undertake will be for and on behalf of others. You can be proud, and on some occasions even haughty, and yet you are also regal in your bearing and honest to the point of absurdity. Nobody could doubt your sincerity,

Leo and its Ascendants

and you have the soul of a poet combined with the bravery of a lion.

All of this is good, but it makes you rather difficult to approach, unless the person in question has first adopted a crouching and subservient attitude. Not that you would wish them to do so. It's simply that the impression you give and the motivation that underpins it are two quite different things. You are greatly respected, and in the case of those individuals who know your real nature, you are also deeply loved. But life would be much simpler if you didn't always have to fight the wars that those around you are happy to start. Relaxation is a word you don't really understand and you would be doing yourself a favour if you looked it up in a dictionary.

Leo with Taurus Ascendant

Oh dear, this can be rather a hedonistic combination. The trouble is that Taurus tends to have a great sense of what looks and feels right, whilst Leo, being a Cat, is inclined to preen itself on almost any occasion. The combination tends towards self-love, which is all too likely for someone who is perfect. But don't be too dispirited about these facts, because there is a great deal going for you in other ways. For a start you have one of the warmest hearts to be found anywhere, and you are so brave that others marvel at the courage you display. The mountains that you climb may not be of the large, rocky sort, but you manage to find plenty of pinnacles to scale all the same, and you invariably get to the top.

Routines might bore you a little more than would be the case with Taurus alone, but you don't mind being alone. Why should you? You are probably the nicest person you know! Thus if you were ever to be cast up on a deserted island you would people the place all on your own, and there would never be any crime, untidiness or arguments. Problems only arise when other people are involved. However, in social settings you are charming, good to know and full of ideas that really have legs. You preserve your youth well into middle age but at base you can tend to worry more than is good for you.

Leo with Gemini Ascendant

Many Gemini people think about doing great things, whilst those who enjoy a Leo Sun do much more than simply think. You have the intrepid qualities of Gemini, but you always keep a sense of humour and are especially good to be around. Bold and quite fearless, you are inclined to go where nobody has gone before, no matter if this is into a precarious business venture or up a mountain that has not been previously climbed. It is people such as you who first explored the world, and you love to know what lies around the next corner and over the far hill.

Kind and loving, you are especially loyal to your friends and would do almost anything on their behalf. As a result they show the greatest concern for you too. However, there are times when the Cat walks alone, and you are probably better at being on your own than would often be the case for the typical Gemini subject. In many way you are fairly self-contained and don't tend to get bored too much unless you are forced to do the same things time and time again. You have a great sense of fun, could talk to just about anyone and usually greet the world with a big smile.

Leo with Cancer Ascendant

This can be a very fortunate combination, for when seen at its best it brings all the concern and the natural caring qualities of Cancer, allied to the more dynamic and very brave face of Leo. Somehow there is a great deal of visible energy here but it manifests itself in a way that always shows a concern for the world at large. No matter what charitable works are going on in your district, it is likely that you will be involved in one way or another, and you relish the cut and thrust of life much more than the retiring side of Cancer would seem to do. You are quite capable of walking alone and don't really need the company of others for large chunks of the average day. However, when you are in social situations you fare very well and can usually be observed with a smile on your face.

Conversationally speaking you have sound, considered opinions and often represent the voice of steady wisdom when faced with a situation that calls for arbitration. In fact you will often be put in this situation and there is more than one politician and union representative who shares this undeniably powerful zodiac combination. Like all those associated with the sign of Cancer you love to travel and can make a meal out of your journeys, with brave, intrepid Leo lending a hand in the planning and the doing.

THE MOON AND THE PART IT PLAYS IN YOUR LIFE

In astrology the Moon is probably the single most important heavenly body after the Sun. Its unique position, as partner to the Earth on its journey around the solar system, means that the Moon appears to pass through the signs of the zodiac extremely quickly. The zodiac position of the Moon at the time of your birth plays a great part in personal character and is especially significant in the build-up of your emotional nature.

Sun Moon Cycles

The first lunar cycle deals with the part the position of the Moon plays relative to your Sun sign. I have made the fluctuations of this pattern easy for you to understand by means of a simple cyclic graph. It appears on the first page of each 'Your Month At A Glance', under the title 'Highs and Lows'. The graph displays the lunar cycle and you will soon learn to understand how its movements have a bearing on your level of energy and your abilities.

Your Own Moon Sign

Discovering the position of the Moon at the time of your birth has always been notoriously difficult because tracking the complex zodiac positions of the Moon is not easy. This process has been reduced to three simple stages with Old Moore's unique Lunar Tables. A breakdown of the Moon's zodiac positions can be found from page 28 onwards, so that once you know what your Moon Sign is, you can see what part this plays in the overall build-up of your personal character.

If you follow the instructions on the next page you will soon be able to work out exactly what zodiac sign the Moon occupied on the day that you were born and you can then go on to compare the reading for this position with those of your Sun sign and your Ascendant. It is partly the comparison between these three important positions that goes towards making you the unique individual you are.

HOW TO DISCOVER YOUR MOON SIGN

This is a three-stage process. You may need a pen and a piece of paper but if you follow the instructions below the process should only take a minute or so.

STAGE 1 First of all you need to know the Moon Age at the time of your birth. If you look at Moon Table 1, on page 26, you will find all the years between 1917 and 2015 down the left side. Find the year of your birth and then trace across to the right to the month of your birth. Where the two intersect you will find a number. This is the date of the New Moon in the month that you were born. You now need to count forward the number of days between the New Moon and your own birthday. For example, if the New Moon in the month of your birth was shown as being the 6th and you were born on the 20th, your Moon Age Day would be 14. If the New Moon in the month of your birth came after your birthday, you need to count forward from the New Moon in the previous month. If you were born in a Leap Year, remember to count the 29th February. You can tell if your birth year was a Leap Year if the last two digits can be divided by four. Whatever the result, jot this number down so that you do not forget it.

STAGE 2 Take a look at Moon Table 2 on page 27. Down the left hand column look for the date of your birth. Now trace across to the month of your birth. Where the two meet you will find a letter. Copy this letter down alongside your Moon Age Day.

STAGE 3 Moon Table 3 on page 27 will supply you with the zodiac sign the Moon occupied on the day of your birth. Look for your Moon Age Day down the left hand column and then for the letter you found in Stage 2. Where the two converge you will find a zodiac sign and this is the sign occupied by the Moon on the day that you were born.

Your Zodiac Moon Sign Explained

You will find a profile of all zodiac Moon Signs on pages 00 to 00, showing in yet another way how astrology helps to make you into the individual that you are. In each daily entry of the Astral Diary you can find the zodiac position of the Moon for every day of the year. This also allows you to discover your lunar birthdays. Since the Moon passes through all the signs of the zodiac in about a month, you can expect something like twelve lunar birthdays each year. At these times you are likely to be emotionally steady and able to make the sort of decisions that have real, lasting value.

Moon Table 1

Moon Table 1

YEAR	JUN	JUL	AUG	YEAR	JUN	JUL	AUG	YEAR	JUN	JUL	AUG
1917	19	18	17	1950	15	15	13	1983	11	10	8
1918	8	8	6	1951	4	4	2	1984	29	28	26
1919	27	27	25	1952	22	22	20	1985	18	17	16
1920	16	15	14	1953	11	11	9	1986	7	7	5
1921	6	5	3	1954	1/30	29	28	1987	26	25	24
1922	25	24	22	1955	20	19	17	1988	14	13	12
1923	14	14	12	1956	8	8	6	1989	3	3	1/31
1924	2	2/31	30	1957	27	27	25	1990	22	22	20
1925	21	20	19	1958	17	16	15	1991	11	11	9
1926	10	9	8	1959	6	6	4	1992	1/30	29	28
1927	29	28	27	1960	24	24	22	1993	20	19	17
1928	18	17	16	1961	13	12	11	1994	9	8	7
1929	7	6	5	1962	2	1/31	30	1995	27	27	26
1930	26	25	24	1963	21	20	19	1996	17	15	14
1931	16	15	13	1964	10	9	7	1997	5	4	3
1932	4	3	2/31	1965	29	28	26	1998	24	23	22
1933	23	22	21	1966	18	17	16	1999	13	13	11
1934	12	11	10	1967	7	7	5	2000	2	1/31	29
1935	1/30	30	29	1968	26	25	24	2001	21	20	19
1936	19	18	17	1969	14	13	12	2002	10	9	8
1937	8	8	6	1970	4	4	2	2003	29	28	27
1938	27	27	25	1971	22	22	20	2004	16	16	15
1939	17	16	15	1972	11	11	9	2005	6	6	4
1940	6	5	4	1973	1/30	29	28	2006	26	25	23
1941	24	24	22	1974	20	19	17	2007	15	15	13
1942	13	13	12	1975	9	9	7	2008	4	3	1/31
1943	2	2	1/30	1976	27	27	25	2009	23	22	20
1944	20	20	18	1977	16	16	14	2010	12	12	10
1945	10	9	8	1978	5	5	4	2011	2	2/31	29
1946	29	28	26	1979	24	24	22	2012	19	19	17
1947	18	17	16	1980	13	12	11	2013	8	7	6
1948	7	6	5	1981	2	1/31	29	2014	27	25	24
1949	26	25	24	1982	21	20	19	2015	17	16	15

Moon Tables 2 and 3

Table 2

DAY	JUL	AUG
1	R	U
2	R	U
3	S	V
4	S	V
5	S	V
6	S	V
7	S	V
8	S	V
9	S	V
10	S	V
11	S	V
12	S	V
13	T	V
14	T	W
15	T	W
16	T	W
17	T	W
18	T	W
19	T	W
20	T	W
21	T	W
22	T	W
23	T	W
24	U	X
25	U	X
26	U	X
27	U	X
28	U	X
29	U	X
30	U	X
31	U	X

Table 3

M/D	R	S	T	U	V	W	X
0	CA	CA	LE	LE	LE	LE	VI
1	CA	LE	LE	LE	VI	VI	VI
2	LE	LE	LE	VI	VI	VI	LI
3	LE	LE	VI	VI	VI	LI	LI
4	LE	VI	VI	LI	LI	LI	LI
5	VI	VI	LI	LI	LI	SC	SC
6	VI	LI	LI	LI	SC	SC	SC
7	LI	LI	LI	SC	SC	SA	SA
8	LI	LI	SC	SC	SC	SA	SA
9	SC	SC	SC	SA	SA	SA	SA
10	SC	SC	SA	SA	SA	CP	CP
11	SA	SA	SA	CP	CP	CP	CP
12	SA	SA	SA	CP	CP	AQ	AQ
13	SA	SA	CP	CP	CP	AQ	AQ
14	CP	CP	CP	AQ	AQ	AQ	PI
15	CP	CP	AQ	AQ	AQ	PI	PI
16	AQ	AQ	AQ	AQ	PI	PI	PI
17	AQ	AQ	AQ	PI	PI	PI	AR
18	AQ	AQ	PI	PI	PI	AR	AR
19	PI	PI	PI	PI	AR	AR	AR
20	PI	PI	AR	AR	AR	TA	TA
21	PI	AR	AR	AR	TA	TA	TA
22	AR	AR	AR	TA	TA	TA	GE
23	AR	AR	TA	TA	TA	GE	GE
24	AR	TA	TA	TA	GE	GE	GE
25	TA	TA	GE	GE	GE	CA	CA
26	TA	GE	GE	GE	CA	CA	CA
27	GE	GE	GE	CA	CA	CA	LE
28	GE	GE	CA	CA	CA	LE	LE
29	GE	CA	CA	CA	LE	LE	LE

AR = Aries, TA = Taurus, GE = Gemini, CA = Cancer, LE = Leo, VI = Virgo, LI = Libra, SC = Scorpio, SA = Sagittarius, CP = Capricorn, AQ = Aquarius, PI = Pisces

MOON SIGNS

Moon in Aries

You have a strong imagination, courage, determination and a desire to do things in your own way and forge your own path through life.

Originality is a key attribute; you are seldom stuck for ideas although your mind is changeable and you could take the time to focus on individual tasks. Often quick-tempered, you take orders from few people and live life at a fast pace. Avoid health problems by taking regular time out for rest and relaxation.

Emotionally, it is important that you talk to those you are closest to and work out your true feelings. Once you discover that people are there to help, there is less necessity for you to do everything yourself.

Moon in Taurus

The Moon in Taurus gives you a courteous and friendly manner, which means you are likely to have many friends.

The good things in life mean a lot to you, as Taurus is an Earth sign that delights in experiences which please the senses. Hence you are probably a lover of good food and drink, which may in turn mean you need to keep an eye on the bathroom scales, especially as looking good is also important to you.

Emotionally you are fairly stable and you stick by your own standards. Taureans do not respond well to change. Intuition also plays an important part in your life.

Moon in Gemini

You have a warm-hearted character, sympathetic and eager to help others. At times reserved, you can also be articulate and chatty: this is part of the paradox of Gemini, which always brings duplicity to the nature. You are interested in current affairs, have a good intellect, and are good company and likely to have many friends. Most of your friends have a high opinion of you and would be ready to defend you should the need arise. However, this is usually unnecessary, as you are quite capable of defending yourself in any verbal confrontation.

Travel is important to your inquisitive mind and you find intellectual stimulus in mixing with people from different cultures. You also gain much from reading, writing and the arts but you do need plenty of rest and relaxation in order to avoid fatigue.

Moon in Cancer

The Moon in Cancer at the time of birth is a fortunate position as Cancer is the Moon's natural home. This means that the qualities of compassion and understanding given by the Moon are especially enhanced in your nature, and you are friendly and sociable and cope well with emotional pressures. You cherish home and family life, and happily do the domestic tasks. Your surroundings are important to you and you hate squalor and filth. You are likely to have a love of music and poetry.

Your basic character, although at times changeable like the Moon itself, depends on symmetry. You aim to make your surroundings comfortable and harmonious, for yourself and those close to you.

Moon in Leo

The best qualities of the Moon and Leo come together to make you warmhearted, fair, ambitious and self-confident. With good organisational abilities, you invariably rise to a position of responsibility in your chosen career. This is fortunate as you don't enjoy being an 'also-ran' and would rather be an important part of a small organisation than a menial in a large one.

You should be lucky in love, and happy, provided you put in the effort to make a comfortable home for yourself and those close to you. It is likely that you will have a love of pleasure, sport, music and literature. Life brings you many rewards, most of them as a direct result of your own efforts, although you may be luckier than average and ready to make the best of any situation.

Moon in Virgo

You are endowed with good mental abilities and a keen receptive memory, but you are never ostentatious or pretentious. Naturally quite reserved, you still have many friends, especially of the opposite sex. Marital relationships must be discussed carefully and worked at so that they remain harmonious, as personal attachments can be a problem if you do not give them your full attention.

Talented and persevering, you possess artistic qualities and are a good homemaker. Earning your honours through genuine merit, you work long and hard towards your objectives but show little pride in your achievements. Many short journeys will be undertaken in your life.

Moon Signs

Moon in Libra

With the Moon in Libra you are naturally popular and make friends easily. People like you, probably more than you realise, you bring fun to a party and are a natural diplomat. For all its good points, Libra is not the most stable of astrological signs and, as a result, your emotions can be a little unstable too. Therefore, although the Moon in Libra is said to be good for love and marriage, your Sun sign and Rising sign will have an important effect on your emotional and loving qualities.

You must remember to relate to others in your decision-making. Co-operation is crucial because Libra represents the 'balance' of life that can only be achieved through harmonious relationships. Conformity is not easy for you because Libra, an Air sign, likes its independence.

Moon in Scorpio

Some people might call you pushy. In fact, all you really want to do is to live life to the full and protect yourself and your family from the pressures of life. Take care to avoid giving the impression of being sarcastic or impulsive and use your energies wisely and constructively.

You have great courage and you invariably achieve your goals by force of personality and sheer effort. You are fond of mystery and are good at predicting the outcome of situations and events. Travel experiences can be beneficial to you.

You may experience problems if you do not take time to examine your motives in a relationship, and also if you allow jealousy, always a feature of Scorpio, to cloud your judgement.

Moon in Sagittarius

The Moon in Sagittarius helps to make you a generous individual with humanitarian qualities and a kind heart. Restlessness may be intrinsic as your mind is seldom still. Perhaps because of this, you have a need for change that could lead you to several major moves during your adult life. You are not afraid to stand your ground when you know your judgement is right, you speak directly and have good intuition.

At work you are quick, efficient and versatile and so you make an ideal employee. You need work to be intellectually demanding and do not enjoy tedious routines.

In relationships, you anger quickly if faced with stupidity or deception, though you are just as quick to forgive and forget. Emotionally, there are times when your heart rules your head.

Moon in Capricorn

The Moon in Capricorn makes you popular and likely to come into the public eye in some way. The watery Moon is not entirely comfortable in the Earth sign of Capricorn and this may lead to some difficulties in the early years of life. An initial lack of creative ability and indecision must be overcome before the true qualities of patience and perseverance inherent in Capricorn can show through.

You have good administrative ability and are a capable worker, and if you are careful you can accumulate wealth. But you must be cautious and take professional advice in partnerships, as you are open to deception. You may be interested in social or welfare work, which suit your organisational skills and sympathy for others.

Moon in Aquarius

The Moon in Aquarius makes you an active and agreeable person with a friendly, easy-going nature. Sympathetic to the needs of others, you flourish in a laid-back atmosphere. You are broad-minded, fair and open to suggestion, although sometimes you have an unconventional quality which others can find hard to understand.

You are interested in the strange and curious, and in old articles and places. You enjoy trips to these places and gain much from them. Political, scientific and educational work interests you and you might choose a career in science or technology.

Money-wise, you make gains through innovation and concentration and Lunar Aquarians often tackle more than one job at a time. In love you are kind and honest.

Moon in Pisces

You have a kind, sympathetic nature, somewhat retiring at times, but you always take account of others' feelings and help when you can.

Personal relationships may be problematic, but as life goes on you can learn from your experiences and develop a better understanding of yourself and the world around you.

You have a fondness for travel, appreciate beauty and harmony and hate disorder and strife. You may be fond of literature and would make a good writer or speaker yourself. You have a creative imagination and may come across as an incurable romantic. You have strong intuition, maybe bordering on a mediumistic quality, which sets you apart from the mass. You may not be rich in cash terms, but your personal gifts are worth more than gold.

LEO IN LOVE

Discover how compatible in love you are with people from the same and other signs of the zodiac. Five stars equals a match made in heaven!

Leo meets Leo

More of a mutual appreciation society than a relationship, this is a promising match. Leo is kind, considerate, lofty, idealistic and brave, all qualities which are mirrored by a Leo partner. Both Lions will be determined in their ambitions, recognise the importance of the family and share a mutual love in all areas of their lives. Furthermore, Leo loves to be loved and so will give and receive it in equal amounts. There won't be many arguments but when there are – watch out! Star rating: *****

Leo meets Virgo

There is a chance for this couple, but it won't be trouble-free. Leo and Virgo view life very differently: Virgo is of a serious nature, struggling to relate to Leo's relentless optimism and cheerfulness, and even finding it annoying. Leo, meanwhile, may find Virgo stodgy, sometimes dark, and uninspiring. The saving grace comes through communication – Leo knows how to make Virgo talk, which is what it needs. If this pair find happiness, though, it may be a case of opposites attract! Star rating: ***

Leo meets Libra

The biggest drawback here is likely to be in the issue of commitment. Leo knows everything about constancy and faithfulness, a lesson which, sadly, Libra needs to learn. Librans are easy-going and diplomatic, qualities which are useful when Leo is on the war-path. This couple should be compatible on a personal level and any problems tend to relate to the different way in which these signs deal with outside factors. With good will and an open mind, it can work out well enough. Star rating: ***

Leo meets Scorpio

Stand back and watch the sparks fly! Scorpio has the deep sensitivity of a Water sign but it is also partially ruled by Fire planet Mars, from which it draws a great power that Leo will find difficult. Leo loves to take charge and really hates to feel psychologically undermined, which is Scorpio's stock-in-trade. Scorpio may find Leo's ideals a little shallow, which will be upsetting to the Lion. Anything is possible, but this possibility is rather slimmer than most. Star rating: **

Leo meets Sagittarius

An excellent match, as Leo and Sagittarius have so much in common. Their general approach to life is very similar, although as they are both Fire signs they can clash impressively! Sagittarius is shallower and more flippant than Leo likes to think of itself, and the Archer will be the one taking emotional chances. Sagittarius has met its match in the Lion's den, as brave Leo won't be outdone by anyone. Financially, they will either be very wealthy or struggling, and family life may be chaotic. Problems, like joys, are handled jointly – and that leads to happiness. Star rating: *****

Leo meets Capricorn

Despite promising appearances, this match often fails to thrive. Capricorn focuses on long-term objectives and, like Leo, is very practical. Both signs are capable of attaining success after a great struggle, which while requiring effort, gives them a mutual goal. But when life is easier, the cracks begin to show. Capricorn can be too serious for Leo, and the couple share few ideals. Leo loves luxury, Capricorn seeks austerity. Leo is warm but Capricorn seems cold and wintry in comparison. Both have many good points, but they don't seem to fire each other off properly. Star rating: **

Leo in Love

Leo meets Aquarius

The problem here is that Aquarius doesn't 'think' in the general sense of the word, it 'knows'. Leo, on the other hand, is more practical and relies more on logical reasoning, and consequently it doesn't understand Aquarius very well. Aquarians can also appear slightly frosty in their appreciation of others and this, too, will eventually annoy Leo. This is a good match for a business partnership because Aquarius is astute, while Leo is brave, but personally the prognosis is less promising. Tolerance, understanding and forbearance are all needed to make this work. Star rating: **

Leo meets Pisces

Pisces always needs to understand others, which makes Leo feel warm and loved, while Leo sees, to its delight, that Pisces needs to be protected and taken care of. Pisceans are often lacking in self-confidence, which is something Leo has to spare, and happily it is often infectious. Pisces' inevitable cares are swept away on a tide of Leonine cheerfulness. This couple's home would be cheerful, and full of love which is beneficial to all family members. This is not a meeting of minds, but rather an understanding and appreciation of differences. Star rating: ****

Leo meets Aries

Stand by for action and make sure that the house is sound-proof! Leo is a lofty idealist and there is always likely to be friction when two Fire signs meet. To compensate, there is much mutual admiration, together with a desire to please. Where there are shared incentives, the prognosis is good but it's important not to let little irritations blow up. Both signs want to have their own way and this is a sure cause of trouble. There might not be much patience here, but there is plenty of action. Star rating: *****

Leo meets Taurus

Here we find a generally successful pairing, which frequently leads to an enduring relationship. Taurus needs stimulation which Leo is happy to offer, while Leo responds well to the Bull's sense of order. The essence of the relationship is balance, but it may be achieved with wild swings of the scales on the way, so don't expect a quiet life, though this pair will enjoy a reconciliation after an argument! Material success is probable and, as both like children, a family is likely. Star rating: ***

Leo meets Gemini

There can be problems here, but Gemini is adaptable enough to overcome many of them. Leo is a go-getter and might sometimes rail against Gemini's flighty tendencies, while Gemini's mental disorganisation can undermine Leo's practicality. However, Leo is cheerful and enjoys Gemini's jokey, flippant qualities. At times of personal intimacy, the two signs should be compatible. Leo and Gemini share very high ideals, but Leo will stick at them for longer. Patience is needed on both sides for the relationship to develop. Star rating: ***

Leo meets Cancer

This relationship will usually be directed by dominant Leo more towards its own needs than Cancer's. However, the Crab will willingly play second fiddle to more progressive and bossy types as it is deeply emotional and naturally supportive. Leo is bright, caring, magnanimous and protective and so, as long as it isn't over-assertive, this could be a good match. On the surface, Cancer appears the more conventional of the two, but Leo will discover, to its delight, that underneath it can be unusual and quirky. Star rating: ****

VENUS:
THE PLANET OF LOVE

If you look up at the sky around sunset or sunrise you will often see Venus in close attendance to the Sun. It is arguably one of the most beautiful sights of all and there is little wonder that historically it became associated with the goddess of love. But although Venus does play an important part in the way you view love and in the way others see you romantically, this is only one of the spheres of influence that it enjoys in your overall character.

Venus has a part to play in the more cultured side of your life and has much to do with your appreciation of art, literature, music and general creativity. Even the way you look is responsive to the part of the zodiac that Venus occupied at the start of your life, though this fact is also down to your Sun sign and Ascending sign. If, at the time you were born, Venus occupied one of the more gregarious zodiac signs, you will be more likely to wear your heart on your sleeve, as well as to be more attracted to entertainment, social gatherings and good company. If on the other hand Venus occupied a quiet zodiac sign at the time of your birth, you would tend to be more retiring and less willing to shine in public situations.

It's good to know what part the planet Venus plays in your life, for it can have a great bearing on the way you appear to the rest of the world and since we all have to mix with others, you can learn to make the very best of what Venus has to offer you.

One of the great complications in the past has always been trying to establish exactly what zodiac position Venus enjoyed when you were born, because the planet is notoriously difficult to track. However, I have solved that problem by creating a table that is exclusive to your Sun sign, which you will find on the following page.

Establishing your Venus sign could not be easier. Just look up the year of your birth on the page opposite and you will see a sign of the zodiac. This was the sign that Venus occupied in the period covered by your sign in that year. If Venus occupied more than one sign during the period, this is indicated by the date on which the sign changed, and the name of the new sign. For instance, if you were born in 1970, Venus was in Virgo until the 8th August, after which time it was in Libra. If you were born before 8th August your Venus sign is Virgo, if you were born on or after 8th August, your Venus sign is Libra. Once you have established the position of Venus at the time of your birth, you can then look in the pages which follow to see how this has a bearing on your life as a whole.

Venus: The Planet of Love

1917 LEO / 28.7 VIRGO
1918 LEO / 25.7 VIRGO / 19.8 LIBRA
1919 VIRGO
1920 LEO / 12.8 VIRGO
1921 GEMINI / 6.8 CANCER
1922 VIRGO / 11.8 LIBRA
1923 CANCER / 4.8 LEO
1924 GEMINI / 25.7 CANCER
1925 LEO / 28.7 VIRGO
1926 LEO / 24.7 VIRGO / 18.8 LIBRA
1927 VIRGO
1928 LEO / 12.8 VIRGO
1929 GEMINI / 5.8 CANCER
1930 VIRGO / 10.8 LIBRA
1931 CANCER / 3.8 LEO
1932 GEMINI / 28.7 CANCER
1933 LEO / 27.7 VIRGO
1934 LEO / 23.7 VIRGO / 17.8 LIBRA
1935 VIRGO
1936 LEO / 11.8 VIRGO
1937 GEMINI / 5.8 CANCER
1938 VIRGO / 10.8 LIBRA
1939 CANCER / 3.8 LEO
1940 GEMINI / 1.8 CANCER
1941 LEO / 27.7 VIRGO
1942 LEO / 23.7 VIRGO / 17.8 LIBRA
1943 VIRGO
1944 LEO / 11.8 VIRGO
1945 GEMINI / 5.8 CANCER
1946 VIRGO / 9.8 LIBRA
1947 CANCER / 2.8 LEO
1948 GEMINI / 3.8 CANCER
1949 LEO / 26.7 VIRGO
1950 LEO / 23.7 VIRGO / 16.8 LIBRA
1951 VIRGO
1952 LEO / 10.8 VIRGO
1953 GEMINI / 4.8 CANCER
1954 VIRGO / 9.8 LIBRA
1955 CANCER / 1.8 LEO
1956 GEMINI / 4.8 CANCER
1957 LEO / 26.7 VIRGO
1958 VIRGO / 16.8 LIBRA
1959 VIRGO
1960 LEO / 9.8 VIRGO
1961 GEMINI / 4.8 CANCER
1962 VIRGO / 9.8 LIBRA
1963 CANCER / 1.8 LEO
1964 GEMINI / 5.8 CANCER
1965 LEO / 25.7 VIRGO
1966 VIRGO / 16.8 LIBRA
1967 VIRGO
1968 LEO / 9.8 VIRGO
1969 GEMINI / 4.8 CANCER
1970 VIRGO / 8.8 LIBRA

1971 CANCER / 31.7 LEO
1972 GEMINI / 5.8 CANCER
1973 LEO / 25.7 VIRGO
1974 VIRGO / 15.8 LIBRA
1975 VIRGO
1976 LEO / 9.8 VIRGO
1977 GEMINI / 3.8 CANCER
1978 VIRGO / 8.8 LIBRA
1979 CANCER / 31.7 LEO
1980 GEMINI / 6.8 CANCER
1981 LEO / 24.7 VIRGO
1982 VIRGO / 15.8 LIBRA
1983 VIRGO
1984 LEO / 8.8 VIRGO
1985 GEMINI / 3.8 CANCER
1986 VIRGO / 7.8 LIBRA
1987 CANCER / 30.7 LEO
1988 GEMINI / 6.8 CANCER
1989 LEO / 24.7 VIRGO
1990 VIRGO / 14.8 LIBRA
1991 VIRGO / 22.8 LEO
1992 LEO / 8.8 VIRGO
1993 GEMINI / 2.8 CANCER
1994 VIRGO / 7.8 LIBRA
1995 CANCER / 30.7 LEO
1996 GEMINI / 7.8 CANCER
1997 LEO / 24.7 VIRGO
1998 VIRGO / 14.8 LIBRA
1999 VIRGO / 22.8 LEO
2000 LEO / 8.8 VIRGO
2001 GEMINI / 1.8 CANCER
2002 VIRGO / 8.8 LIBRA
2003 CANCER / 30.7 LEO
2004 GEMINI / 7.8 CANCER
2005 LEO / 24.7 VIRGO
2006 VIRGO / 14.8 LIBRA
2007 VIRGO / 22.8 LEO
2008 LEO / 8.8 VIRGO
2009 GEMINI / 1.8 CANCER
2010 VIRGO / 8.8 LIBRA
2011 CANCER / 30.7 LEO
2012 GEMINI / 7.8 CANCER
2013 LEO / 24.7 VIRGO
2014 VIRGO / 14.8 LIBRA
2015 VIRGO / 22.8 LEO

VENUS THROUGH THE ZODIAC SIGNS

Venus in Aries

Amongst other things, the position of Venus in Aries indicates a fondness for travel, music and all creative pursuits. Your nature tends to be affectionate and you would try not to create confusion or difficulty for others if it could be avoided. Many people with this planetary position have a great love of the theatre, and mental stimulation is of the greatest importance. Early romantic attachments are common with Venus in Aries, so it is very important to establish a genuine sense of romantic continuity. Early marriage is not recommended, especially if it is based on sympathy. You may give your heart a little too readily on occasions.

Venus in Taurus

You are capable of very deep feelings and your emotions tend to last for a very long time. This makes you a trusting partner and lover, whose constancy is second to none. In life you are precise and careful and always try to do things the right way. Although this means an ordered life, which you are comfortable with, it can also lead you to be rather too fussy for your own good. Despite your pleasant nature, you are very fixed in your opinions and quite able to speak your mind. Others are attracted to you and historical astrologers always quoted this position of Venus as being very fortunate in terms of marriage. However, if you find yourself involved in a failed relationship, it could take you a long time to trust again.

Venus in Gemini

As with all associations related to Gemini, you tend to be quite versatile, anxious for change and intelligent in your dealings with the world at large. You may gain money from more than one source but you are equally good at spending it. There is an inference here that you are a good communicator, via either the written or the spoken word, and you love to be in the company of interesting people. Always on the look-out for culture, you may also be very fond of music, and love to indulge the curious and cultured side of your nature. In romance you tend to have more than one relationship and could find yourself associated with someone who has previously been a friend or even a distant relative.

Venus through the Zodiac Signs

Venus in Cancer

You often stay close to home because you are very fond of family and enjoy many of your most treasured moments when you are with those you love. Being naturally sympathetic, you will always do anything you can to support those around you, even people you hardly know at all. This charitable side of your nature is your most noticeable trait and is one of the reasons why others are naturally so fond of you. Being receptive and in some cases even psychic, you can see through to the soul of most of those with whom you come into contact. You may not commence too many romantic attachments but when you do give your heart, it tends to be unconditionally.

Venus in Leo

It must become quickly obvious to almost anyone you meet that you are kind, sympathetic and yet determined enough to stand up for anyone or anything that is truly important to you. Bright and sunny, you warm the world with your natural enthusiasm and would rarely do anything to hurt those around you, or at least not intentionally. In romance you are ardent and sincere, though some may find your style just a little overpowering. Gains come through your contacts with other people and this could be especially true with regard to romance, for love and money often come hand in hand for those who were born with Venus in Leo. People claim to understand you, though you are more complex than you seem.

Venus in Virgo

Your nature could well be fairly quiet no matter what your Sun sign might be, though this fact often manifests itself as an inner peace and would not prevent you from being basically sociable. Some delays and even the odd disappointment in love cannot be ruled out with this planetary position, though it's a fact that you will usually find the happiness you look for in the end. Catapulting yourself into romantic entanglements that you know to be rather ill-advised is not sensible, and it would be better to wait before you committed yourself exclusively to any one person. It is the essence of your nature to serve the world at large and through doing so it is possible that you will attract money at some stage in your life.

Venus in Libra

Venus is very comfortable in Libra and bestows upon those people who have this planetary position a particular sort of kindness that is easy to recognise. This is a very good position for all sorts of friendships and also for romantic attachments that usually bring much joy into your life. Few individuals with Venus in Libra would avoid marriage and since you are capable of great depths of love, it is likely that you will find a contented personal life. You like to mix with people of integrity and intelligence but don't take kindly to scruffy surroundings or work that means getting your hands too dirty. Careful speculation, good business dealings and money through marriage all seem fairly likely.

Venus in Scorpio

You are quite open and tend to spend money quite freely, even on those occasions when you don't have very much. Although your intentions are always good, there are times when you get yourself in to the odd scrape and this can be particularly true when it comes to romance, which you may come to late or from a rather unexpected direction. Certainly you have the power to be happy and to make others contented on the way, but you find the odd stumbling block on your journey through life and it could seem that you have to work harder than those around you. As a result of this, you gain a much deeper understanding of the true value of personal happiness than many people ever do, and are likely to achieve true contentment in the end.

Venus in Sagittarius

You are lighthearted, cheerful and always able to see the funny side of any situation. These facts enhance your popularity, which is especially high with members of the opposite sex. You should never have to look too far to find romantic interest in your life, though it is just possible that you might be too willing to commit yourself before you are certain that the person in question is right for you. Part of the problem here extends to other areas of life too. The fact is that you like variety in everything and so can tire of situations that fail to offer it. All the same, if you choose wisely and learn to understand your restless side, then great happiness can be yours.

Venus through the Zodiac Signs

Venus in Capricorn

The most notable trait that comes from Venus in this position is that it makes you trustworthy and able to take on all sorts of responsibilities in life. People are instinctively fond of you and love you all the more because you are always ready to help those who are in any form of need. Social and business popularity can be yours and there is a magnetic quality to your nature that is particularly attractive in a romantic sense. Anyone who wants a partner for a lover, a spouse and a good friend too would almost certainly look in your direction. Constancy is the hallmark of your nature and unfaithfulness would go right against the grain. You might sometimes be a little too trusting.

Venus in Aquarius

This location of Venus offers a fondness for travel and a desire to try out something new at every possible opportunity. You are extremely easy to get along with and tend to have many friends from varied backgrounds, classes and inclinations. You like to live a distinct sort of life and gain a great deal from moving about, both in a career sense and with regard to your home. It is not out of the question that you could form a romantic attachment to someone who comes from far away or be attracted to a person of a distinctly artistic and original nature. What you cannot stand is jealousy, for you have friends of both sexes and would want to keep things that way.

Venus in Pisces

The first thing people tend to notice about you is your wonderful, warm smile. Being very charitable by nature you will do anything to help others, even if you don't know them well. Much of your life may be spent sorting out situations for other people, but it is very important to feel that you are living for yourself too. In the main, you remain cheerful, and tend to be quite attractive to members of the opposite sex. Where romantic attachments are concerned, you could be drawn to people who are significantly older or younger than yourself or to someone with a unique career or point of view. It might be best for you to avoid marrying whilst you are still very young.

HOW THE DIAGRAMS WORK

Through the picture diagrams in the Astral Diary I want to help you to plot your year. With them you can see where the positive and negative aspects will be found in each month. To make the most of them, all you have to do is remember where and when!

Let me show you how they work ...

THE MONTH AT A GLANCE

Just as there are twelve separate zodiac signs, so astrologers believe that each sign has twelve separate aspects to life. Each of the twelve segments relates to a different personal aspect. I list them all every month so that their meanings are always clear.

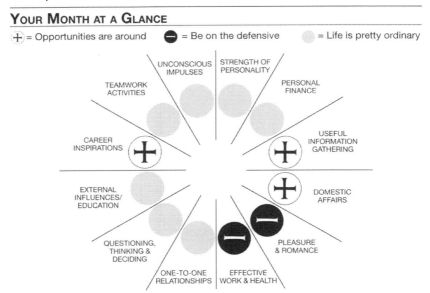

I have designed this chart to show you how and when these twelve different aspects are being influenced throughout the year. When there is a shaded circle, nothing out of the ordinary is to be expected. However, when a circle turns white with a plus sign, the influence is positive. Where the circle is black with a minus sign, it is a negative.

How the Diagrams Work

YOUR ENERGY RHYTHM CHART

Below is a picture diagram in which I link your zodiac group to the rhythm of the Moon. In doing this I have calculated when you will be gaining strength from its influence and equally when you may be weakened by it.

If you think of yourself as being like the tides of the ocean then you may understand how your own energies must also rise and fall. And if you understand how it works and when it is working, then you can better organise your activities to achieve more and get things done more easily.

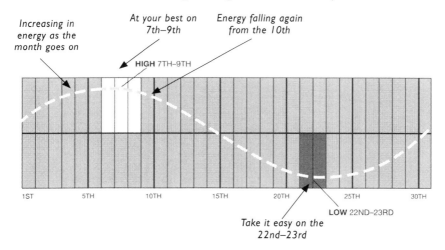

THE KEY DAYS

Some of the entries are in **bold**, which indicates the working of astrological cycles in your life. Look out for them each week as they are the best days to take action or make decisions. The daily text tells you which area of your life to focus on.

MERCURY RETROGRADE

The Mercury symbol (☿) indicates that Mercury is retrograde on that day. Since Mercury governs communication, the fact that it appears to be moving backwards when viewed from the Earth at this time should warn you that your communication skills are not likely to be at their best and you could expect some setbacks.

43

LEO: YOUR YEAR IN BRIEF

You can look forward to a busy and productive year which, though it might not bring your heart's desire, can get you closer to it. You need to be right on the ball from the start of January in order to ride the positive astrological trends that begin the year with possible financial gains and freedom. February continues these trends, but could bring a little confusion, mainly because of the attitudes and ideas of others. Love is important towards the end of February.

With the arrival of the spring and the month of March, you really begin to move forwards. The better weather and longer days will suit you and your confidence grows with the daffodils. Creative potential is especially good around this period, and by April you will be turning this to your advantage, as well as getting on much better in group situations. April may also offer financial improvements and also brings you to a better understanding of past issues.

By the time the early summer arrives, you want to spread your wings and to make as much progress as you can through travel and diversity of any sort. May is best for a change of job and also offers a huge range of possibilities that you will enjoy. In June, you may once again be travelling and you should notice that you are elevated in the minds of people you probably didn't think liked you all that much. Standing up for yourself is especially easy at this time.

July and August should find you generally in the pink and anxious to push forwards on all fronts. This is the time of the year that suits you very well and you shouldn't have any problem getting others to follow your lead. The most regal and noble qualities of Leo are showing at this time, which could increase your popularity and perhaps offer the chance to get your own way. Look out for people who have a definite desire to help you in all sorts of areas of your life.

As the summer draws to a close, you really come into your own. September and October are the two months that really work for you in almost every way, especially so during the first half of October. Concentrated effort is called for and romance could take a turn for the better. Money is likely to come from unexpected directions.

November finds you once again in a go-ahead frame of mind and allies you to likeminded people, some of whom will be extremely useful. Even by the start of December you will be thinking about the Christmas period, which should turn out to be happy, contented and quite old fashioned for many Lions. As you look back over the year, you may realise that you have moved on significantly in many ways.

Your Month at a Glance

⊕ = Opportunities are around　　⊖ = Be on the defensive　　○ = Life is pretty ordinary

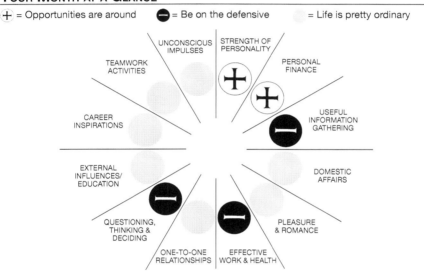

January Highs and Lows

Here I show you how the rhythms of the Moon will affect you this month. Like the tide, your energies and abilities will rise and fall with its pattern. When it is above the centre line, go for it, when it is below, you should be resting.

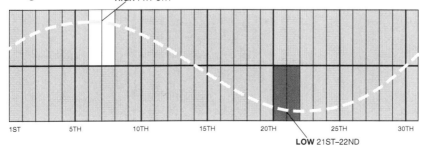

Your Daily Guide to January 2015

1 THURSDAY
Moon Age Day 11   Moon Sign Taurus

Getting out and about now should be very rewarding. You are in a good position to get what you want, particularly in a romantic sense. The attitude of a friend might puzzle you somewhat and it would be sensible to ask a few leading questions before you fire from the hip, as Leo people are inclined to do.

2 FRIDAY
Moon Age Day 12   Moon Sign Gemini

You show great dynamism right now, particularly with regard to your career. If you are a student, you should find that your studies come very easily to you at the moment and virtually all Leo people will be monitoring a very definite improvement in terms of personal popularity. Don't be surprised if someone wants to know you better.

3 SATURDAY
Moon Age Day 13   Moon Sign Gemini

You may have got out of the habit of a particular task or set of jobs that you know to be very important. This Saturday offers you the chance to look at them again and to get on side with a person who hasn't been all that easy to deal with of late. You will be amazed at just how much you can get done.

4 SUNDAY
Moon Age Day 14   Moon Sign Gemini

Getting yourself organised is what life is really about today. Confidence is high and you are able to tell the whole world what you want, and how you intend to go about getting it. There may be necessary changes in the pipeline, but this is no time to be shying away from any of them.

5 MONDAY
Moon Age Day 15   Moon Sign Cancer

Your mental processes are sharp and the more you find yourself in open discussion with others, the better they are likely to be. The real Leo grit is evident and it is highly unlikely that anyone will get in your way. Something you have been looking forward to might not prove quite as interesting or rewarding as you had hoped.

6 TUESDAY
Moon Age Day 16   Moon Sign Cancer

Spend time carefully mulling over anything you hear right now in connection with your work. You don't generally listen to gossip all that much, but for the next couple of days you might hear something useful. The deeper, more spiritual side of Leo is now on display, which might surprise a few people.

Your Daily Guide to January 2015

7 WEDNESDAY
Moon Age Day 17 Moon Sign Leo

Look around carefully, because nobody is better at making the best of opportunities than you are right now. Not everything you want will be forthcoming, but when it isn't, you may simply have yourself to blame. In the best of all worlds, you will usually only have to ask for what you want before it comes your way.

8 THURSDAY
Moon Age Day 18 Moon Sign Leo

Getting others round to your way of thinking is an absolute piece of cake right now, which is why you are getting on so well. There might be someone about who you don't trust. However, your intuition is so strong at the moment that it is unlikely you would have the wool pulled over your eyes.

9 FRIDAY
Moon Age Day 19 Moon Sign Virgo

When it comes to any sort of practical task, it appears you have all the help you could possibly need today. Of course, you might have to open your mouth and say what you need, but that doesn't come at all hard to you. Concentrate on the most important matters early in the day and enjoy yourself later.

10 SATURDAY
Moon Age Day 20 Moon Sign Virgo

A rather busy phase finds you too stressed to take full advantage of some of the opportunities that the weekend offers. Could it be that you are bringing your work home with you or else thinking about it so much you simply fail to register many of the social offers and opportunities that come your way?

11 SUNDAY
Moon Age Day 21 Moon Sign Virgo

There are gains coming your way, even if you are not particularly looking for them. What does work out well for you at present is listening to the advice of people you really rate. On the other hand, you will be staying right away from individuals you find tedious or tiresome.

12 MONDAY
Moon Age Day 22 Moon Sign Libra

Take advantage of current influences to get things done. This could be something of a chore if others accuse you of being too smart for your own good. All the same, you need to plough your own furrow, even if this means getting on the wrong side of someone who is really important to you.

Your Daily Guide to January 2015

13 TUESDAY
Moon Age Day 23 Moon Sign Libra

There are rewarding times in store and all you really have to do to make the most of them is to be in the right place at the right time. Intuition helps again, leading to a time that offers a great deal of variety and the chance to make impressions on people who could prove to be important later.

14 WEDNESDAY
Moon Age Day 24 Moon Sign Scorpio

If you take chances today, choose them carefully. Risks are fine, just as long as they are calculated. Leo is sometimes inclined to push matters just for the sake of doing so, though behaving in this manner at the moment won't get you very far at all and might lead to a degree of confusion you could do without.

15 THURSDAY
Moon Age Day 25 Moon Sign Scorpio

You want to be a freewheeler today, but it might not be all that easy. There is a long way to go in a particular issue, which is why it would be very sensible to hold back for a while. You should not have to look too far to find romance. It might be around the next corner, or even within your own home environment.

16 FRIDAY
Moon Age Day 26 Moon Sign Scorpio

There could be many lighthearted moments in your social life right now. Many of you will be quite pleased to be in a long-term settled relationship and there is likely to be a strong commitment towards the future. Not everyone is your friend, but don't worry about that for now.

17 SATURDAY
Moon Age Day 27 Moon Sign Sagittarius

Romance and personal relationships generally should seem quite harmonious today, especially as you may have more time to look at them. By tomorrow, it's action all the way again, which is exactly why you should enjoy the less stressful moments that surround you now. Look up someone you haven't seen for a while.

18 SUNDAY
Moon Age Day 28 Moon Sign Sagittarius

This is an excellent time for making new friends, as well as for consolidating friendships that already exist. You are taking a fresh and original attitude towards life in general and would be unlikely to show any sort of animosity or meanness of spirit around this period.

Your Daily Guide to January 2015

19 MONDAY
Moon Age Day 29 Moon Sign Capricorn

You are feeling very organised today, you might not take too kindly to other people coming along and making changes to matters that are already settled in your mind. Sharing responsibility is therefore not easy for you now and you will have to work hard to show the more diplomatic qualities you possess.

20 TUESDAY
Moon Age Day 0 Moon Sign Capricorn

There ought to be a wonderfully supportive element from loved ones today, which can make for a very interesting sort of period. Most of the people you meet have something good to say about you and one or two comments are specifically designed to make you feel good. Accept the compliments with humility.

21 WEDNESDAY
Moon Age Day 1 Moon Sign Aquarius

Progress now slows, as the lunar low inclines you to stand and watch, rather than getting involved to your normal extent. There is an opportunity to get ahead but this is born out of patience and thought, rather than action. The mood of today probably goes against the grain, as far as you are concerned – but remember that it is temporary.

22 THURSDAY
Moon Age Day 2 Moon Sign Aquarius

Don't take all the world's troubles on to your own shoulders. You will get ahead far better if you take things steadily and deal with issues that arise one at a time. Romance could be the best place to look for comfort and reassurance – even if you find yourself in the arms of someone rather surprising.

23 FRIDAY
Moon Age Day 3 Moon Sign Pisces

Matters at work should move ahead a good deal quicker today. Life is eventful, so much so that even your quick mind has slight problems keeping up with events. Rules and regulations won't please you all that much and you could be inclined to be somewhat rebellious in small ways.

24 SATURDAY ☿
Moon Age Day 4 Moon Sign Pisces

A time of mental and physical efficiency is at hand, so you can expect the start of the weekend to be quite dynamic. Although you won't find everyone to be equally co-operative at this time, you do have what it takes to build a good team spirit, which extends far into the day.

Your Daily Guide to January 2015

25 SUNDAY ☿   *Moon Age Day 5   Moon Sign Aries*

Though your self-confidence is far from low, you might lack that final spark that makes all the difference when it comes to making important decisions. If this turns out to be the case, rely on the judgement of someone whom you know you can always trust.

26 MONDAY ☿   *Moon Age Day 6   Moon Sign Aries*

There can be a few financial ups and downs today, though in a general sense you ought to find life turning more progressive as the week advances. Take the chance for a change of scenery and don't be too quick to deal with domestic issues, particularly alterations you might want to make at home.

27 TUESDAY ☿   *Moon Age Day 7   Moon Sign Taurus*

You appear to have a strong desire to wander today. Leo is sometimes inclined to feel restricted by circumstances, and the more so at this time of year. If you can't get away in a physical sense, you can at least feed your mind with plans for travel. Personal relationships should be turning out fine.

28 WEDNESDAY ☿   *Moon Age Day 8   Moon Sign Taurus*

An emotionally challenging time is at hand, though this doesn't mean today fails to be enjoyable. You desire at least a little upheaval in your life and certainly would not back down at present in any sort of discussion. At the same time, you are warm, particularly in a romantic sense.

29 THURSDAY   *Moon Age Day 9   Moon Sign Gemini*

This would be a wonderful time for all intimate matters and for getting on side with someone you haven't seen eye to eye with of late. If this individual is also your lover, then you have the chance to be as close to that person as you have ever been. Don't be too quick to jump to conclusions.

30 FRIDAY ☿   *Moon Age Day 10   Moon Sign Gemini*

It is likely that simple friendships will take centre stage today, even above one-to-one attachments. You have a natural desire to keep life uncomplicated and bright. Your instinctive humour means that almost everyone will take delight in your company and will actively single you out for special attention.

Your Daily Guide to January 2015

31 SATURDAY ☿

Moon Age Day 11 Moon Sign Gemini

Someone has the ability to take the wind out of your sails regarding a decision he or she decides to make at the moment. It would be best to avoid getting involved in any grand new deals for the moment. Take care, because not everyone in your vicinity is working on your behalf.

February 2015

Your Month at a Glance

⊕ = Opportunities are around   ⊖ = Be on the defensive   ● = Life is pretty ordinary

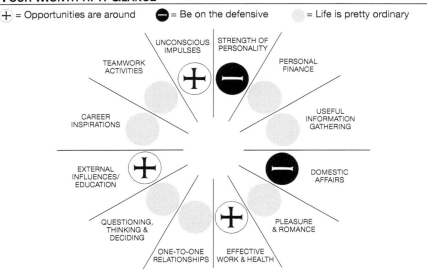

February Highs and Lows

Here I show you how the rhythms of the Moon will affect you this month. Like the tide, your energies and abilities will rise and fall with its pattern. When it is above the centre line, go for it, when it is below, you should be resting.

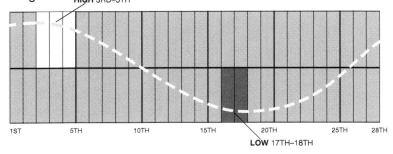

Your Daily Guide to February 2015

1 SUNDAY ☿ *Moon Age Day 12 Moon Sign Cancer*

General routines distract you from ideas you know to be revolutionary and stimulating today. Once again, it is very necessary to look carefully at what the day requires and to leave alone those jobs that are not at all necessary. Avoid becoming bored at all costs. Use your intuition when assessing others.

2 MONDAY ☿ *Moon Age Day 13 Moon Sign Cancer*

Today could be quite sluggish in a professional sense, which is why you are now much more likely to rely on the help and support of those around you. Concentrate on matters that you know to be of supreme importance and leave the dross until another day. In your spare moments, you might choose to read.

3 TUESDAY ☿ *Moon Age Day 14 Moon Sign Leo*

Due to high levels of mental and physical energy, you are now better able to burn the candle at both ends, though only up to a point. There are possible gains due to the part others play in your life. In social or business situations, you can show yourself to be inspirational and powerful.

4 WEDNESDAY ☿ *Moon Age Day 15 Moon Sign Leo*

With a marked boost to your personal energies, this midweek period could prove to be the best so far this year. Although the winter weather might prevent you from going far, you will still be in the mood to travel if you can. Leo is amongst the most intrepid of all the zodiac signs and you show this fact at present.

5 THURSDAY ☿ *Moon Age Day 16 Moon Sign Leo*

A word in the right ear could go a long way to getting you what you want from life. The lunar high presents you with new and improved chances to get ahead. You show a preference for people who are very similar in nature to yourself, but there is just the slightest chance that you might prove contrary in personal matters.

6 FRIDAY ☿ *Moon Age Day 17 Moon Sign Virgo*

Do your very best to establish new social contacts this week, starting today. When it comes to words of love, you are dredging more up than an 18th-century poet! This is slightly unusual behaviour for Leo, so you could shock your partner or someone else dear to your heart.

Your Daily Guide to February 2015

7 SATURDAY ☿ *Moon Age Day 18 Moon Sign Virgo*

You make very entertaining company at present. You are outgoing enough to be fun, yet you show a really sensitive side that others don't always see but that they really like. You might find that you lack confidence when there are important decisions that simply have to be made.

8 SUNDAY ☿ *Moon Age Day 19 Moon Sign Libra*

Pleasant experiences on the social front make for an entertaining time and should leave you feeling that life is more than worthwhile. Unfortunately, not everyone is in quite in the same frame of mind as you and a degree of patience is necessary when dealing with folk who simply won't be happy.

9 MONDAY ☿ *Moon Age Day 20 Moon Sign Libra*

Not all your ambitions are working out quite as you would have wished. It is very important to deal with situations as they arise. If you do this, it is quite possible to make positive strides, even against prevailing circumstances. Above all, show yourself to be as flexible as possible.

10 TUESDAY ☿ *Moon Age Day 21 Moon Sign Libra*

This is definitely the best time to broaden your personal horizons. You can do this by carefully watching what is going on around you. Many of the ideas you have are a great deal better than those of people around you. Convincing them that you know best ought to be a piece of cake if you remain calm.

11 WEDNESDAY ☿ *Moon Age Day 22 Moon Sign Scorpio*

Slowly but surely, your practical skills are beginning to show themselves more fully. Step by careful step, you are able to get ahead and to convince those around you that you know what you are doing. In terms of money, now is the time to begin taking the odd chance because calculated risks pay off.

12 THURSDAY ☿ *Moon Age Day 23 Moon Sign Scorpio*

Group encounters interest you greatly, though you might have to reorder your schedule somewhat in order to get the best from them. If you don't have time to do everything that seems to be necessary, you could try delegating. This isn't always easy for your zodiac sign, but is sometimes necessary.

Your Daily Guide to February 2015

13 FRIDAY ☿ *Moon Age Day 24 Moon Sign Sagittarius*

A dynamic approach to personal matters once again displays itself at the end of the working week. If you have been toiling away for days, you will now be in a better position to see what you really should be doing. If not, getting yourself fully into gear is going to take a little time.

14 SATURDAY *Moon Age Day 25 Moon Sign Sagittarius*

Be prepared for a brief astrological trend to leave you somewhat muddle-headed today. It would not be sensible to make too many decisions, if you can possibly avoid it. Routines are on your mind, even if you try to shirk them, and it might be better simply to get them out of the way, leaving the decks cleared for action.

15 SUNDAY *Moon Age Day 26 Moon Sign Capricorn*

Romantically speaking, today could be something of a downer, though if you are aware of this in advance you can deal with it quite easily. Don't get into too many clinches, particularly if to do so means making someone jealous. You might prefer to keep your contacts light and casual for now.

16 MONDAY *Moon Age Day 27 Moon Sign Capricorn*

Don't hurry things at work and you can achieve good, sensible results. It is important not to rush your fences at all today and there really is no need. Colleagues and friends alike should prove to be very helpful and probably come up with some ideas to complement those you are having at present.

17 TUESDAY *Moon Age Day 28 Moon Sign Aquarius*

Lower your expectations and dig in for a day or two. If you don't, the lunar low could certainly take the wind out of your sails. As long as you treat this period as a time for rest and reflection, all should be well. What you can't afford to do at the moment is to put yourself out on any ledge.

18 WEDNESDAY *Moon Age Day 29 Moon Sign Aquarius*

Maybe you should not try too hard to gain the ear of colleagues or to influence the outcome of specific events today. You are still not firing on all cylinders and would gain from a short period of limited isolation. You might decide to curl up somewhere with a good book, or better still some sort of puzzle.

Your Daily Guide to February 2015

19 THURSDAY
Moon Age Day 0   Moon Sign Pisces

Your willpower can be constructively channelled into all manner of projects now and there is no doubt that it's a force to be reckoned with. Even small-scale efforts can bring their own successes, so it is worthwhile pushing forward on most fronts. Romance appears to be especially well starred right now.

20 FRIDAY
Moon Age Day 1   Moon Sign Pisces

You can meet people now who have the ability to broaden your own perspectives. All in all, this should be a fairly productive sort of day, with a little adventure likely to be thrown in for good measure. A possible fly in the ointment will be a friend who is clearly in need of more than a little emotional support.

21 SATURDAY
Moon Age Day 2   Moon Sign Aries

On the social front, Leo shows a thirst for freedom and new input during much of the weekend. Just following paths you know to have been made for you won't be of much interest, because the pioneering spirit within you is strong. You can arrive at some quite startling conclusions about a friend.

22 SUNDAY
Moon Age Day 3   Moon Sign Aries

You positively shine in social situations and can be the life and soul of any party that is taking place in your vicinity right now. Confidence is strong and you certainly won't be lacking when it comes to making the most favourable impression imaginable. This could be a very fortunate day.

23 MONDAY
Moon Age Day 4   Moon Sign Aries

You could enjoy considerable success at work at the start of this new week. Don't be too quick to put forward your point of view if you know it will clash with that of someone who has control over part of your life. It isn't your way to suck up to anyone, but a little tact won't cost you much and could bring gains.

24 TUESDAY
Moon Age Day 5   Moon Sign Taurus

This is a day on which you can make good use of your time and energy. Planning ahead is important, too, with the possibility of family meetings that allow you to come to terms with the ideas of others. This time of year isn't your favourite, but you can get ahead despite the cold weather and lack of sunshine.

Your Daily Guide to February 2015

25 WEDNESDAY
Moon Age Day 6 Moon Sign Taurus

You might just discover that it is the right time to capitalise on efforts you made some time ago. Longer term planning has been the key to success for some months past, so you can expect many of the gains around now to have been laid down at some time last year. Romance is offered for Leos who are in the market.

26 THURSDAY
Moon Age Day 7 Moon Sign Gemini

The Sun is now in your solar eighth house, so the next three weeks or so are likely to bring the potential for a number of changes. Some of these could be satisfying, but it is necessary for you to remain flexible and open to suggestions. Colleagues could prove to have a trick or two up their sleeves today.

27 FRIDAY
Moon Age Day 8 Moon Sign Gemini

Both emotional and material affairs may improve today, thanks to the intervention and advice of a loved one. Mental endeavours are favoured around now and communication with almost anyone is the key to greater personal success. During most of today, there is nothing to slow you down.

28 SATURDAY
Moon Age Day 9 Moon Sign Cancer

Your intuition regarding the behaviour and thought processes of others is very strong today and certainly should not be ignored. You are also very forthright when it comes to expressing your opinions, so much so that you can turn a few heads. Maybe a little less reaction and a greater degree of understanding are called for.

March
2015

Your Month at a Glance

(+) = Opportunities are around   (−) = Be on the defensive   ● = Life is pretty ordinary

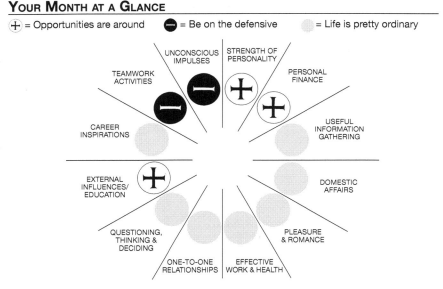

March Highs and Lows

Here I show you how the rhythms of the Moon will affect you this month. Like the tide, your energies and abilities will rise and fall with its pattern. When it is above the centre line, go for it, when it is below, you should be resting.

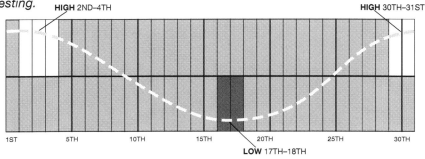

HIGH 2ND–4TH   **HIGH** 30TH–31ST   **LOW** 17TH–18TH

Your Daily Guide to March 2015

1 SUNDAY
Moon Age Day 10   Moon Sign Cancer

A plan of action out there in the competitive world may turn out to be rather less useful that it first appears to be. For this reason, you need to act with circumspection and not to allow your enthusiasm to get the better of you. Avoid confrontation with people who can be of use to you and who are really trying to help.

2 MONDAY
Moon Age Day 11   Moon Sign Leo

Along comes the physical and mental peak right at the beginning of the month. In addition to the lunar high, the Sun is also in a strong position for you, which is bound to bring support and a very cheerful attitude. There is plenty to be done, but the reserves of energy you have at present are deep and enduring.

3 TUESDAY
Moon Age Day 12   Moon Sign Leo

A word in the right ear could see you shifting a host of obstacles today and getting on with things at a good pace. Although not everyone will be on your side at the moment, in the main there is plenty of help when you need it the most. Your attitude is positive and you seem to have a particular penchant for enjoying yourself.

4 WEDNESDAY
Moon Age Day 13   Moon Sign Leo

You won't be able to remain the centre of attention today, but there is a positive side to this state of affairs. If you are not in the limelight, you are far less likely to be criticised, especially for matters that are not really your concern. Refuse to be involved in situations that cannot benefit you in the slightest.

5 THURSDAY
Moon Age Day 14   Moon Sign Virgo

This is a wonderful time for social get-togethers and for showing a very friendly face to the world at large. Now you enjoy a higher personal profile and should not be shy to put your ideas forward. A slightly negative phase for Leo now seems to be at an end and it looks as though your more forceful side is at hand.

6 FRIDAY
Moon Age Day 15   Moon Sign Virgo

Conversation and general communication is key to success at the end of this working week. Although you might think you are saying too much for your own good around now, this really isn't the case. Don't be afraid to put forward an alternative opinion, even when dealing with those who are in charge.

Your Daily Guide to March 2015

7 SATURDAY
Moon Age Day 16   Moon Sign Libra

A more frugal approach to money matters may be both advisable and even necessary. It's really just a case of thinking before you spend lavishly on anything. Keep up your efforts to get ahead generally and don't be frightened to seek the support of people who are in the very best position to lend you a helping hand.

8 SUNDAY
Moon Age Day 17   Moon Sign Libra

Keep an eye out for some good news, which could be coming in from a number of different directions. Communication is favoured, and a long-held ambition could be realised before long. It is also possible that you receive a helping hand from a quite unexpected direction before the day is over.

9 MONDAY
Moon Age Day 18   Moon Sign Libra

Whatever is happening around you now, it is clear that you want to be a part of it. Although there are things going on that demand your attention, you will also be expected to fulfil specific expectations in a family sense. Avoid getting involved in any sort of scheme that you know instinctively might be somewhat shady.

10 TUESDAY
Moon Age Day 19   Moon Sign Scorpio

There is more than a little emphasis on the physical side of life at this time. The Sun is moving on in your chart, towards a fairly inspirational position. Now you feel more progressive and should be looking good. People actively seek you out, especially for social gatherings and you won't be any sort of wallflower at the moment.

11 WEDNESDAY
Moon Age Day 20   Moon Sign Scorpio

If you try to do everything at once you will find that something has to give. Instead, try to pace yourself a little and leave some jobs for other people. There are plenty of folk around at the moment who would be only too willing to lend a hand and you should be humble enough to allow them their moment of glory, too.

12 THURSDAY
Moon Age Day 21   Moon Sign Sagittarius

Everyday discussions have plenty of cut and thrust. You are saying what you think, which is fine as long as you remember that some people are quite sensitive by nature and may not respond well to what you have on your mind. It's important to balance telling the truth as you see it against the possibility of giving offence.

Your Daily Guide to March 2015

13 FRIDAY
Moon Age Day 22   Moon Sign Sagittarius

Today is a career day and a time when you will be addressing the need to push ahead and maybe to gain advancements of some sort. Look out for superiors who are clearly in a position to do you a lot of good and who are simply waiting for you to ask. Confidence is now the key to success in any practical situation.

14 SATURDAY
Moon Age Day 23   Moon Sign Sagittarius

There is a possibility that you will find yourself at odds with others over issues that really don't demand too much attention. If you know you are nitpicking, then it is also clear that you can stop. There are advantages to be gained today simply from being in the right place at the most opportune time.

15 SUNDAY
Moon Age Day 24   Moon Sign Capricorn

Whenever action is the key to success, you are there, champing at the bit. Once again the advice is to move forward carefully and not to overload your nervous system. Problems are there to be solved and that is what you will do. However, some issues probably are not even worth your attention. You need to be selective.

16 MONDAY
Moon Age Day 25   Moon Sign Capricorn

There is a chance that your tendency to be strong willed and determined could get you into some trouble early this week. You might be sure that you are right, but there are always other points of view. It is extremely important at the moment that you stop, look and listen. Information coming from strange directions can be of great assistance.

17 TUESDAY
Moon Age Day 26   Moon Sign Aquarius

The influence of the lunar low could make it difficult to get ahead with practical matters at the moment. Keep a sense of proportion and remain vigilant, but don't try to get ahead too much for today or tomorrow. Keeping your powder dry will pay dividends later.

18 WEDNESDAY
Moon Age Day 27   Moon Sign Aquarius

Although the general quality of life is not sparkling at this time, look for improvements as the day wears on. A little give and take will help a lot, as will spending some time on your own. Confidence begins to increase after lunch and by the evening you could find yourself in the right frame of mind to socialise.

Your Daily Guide to March 2015

19 THURSDAY
Moon Age Day 28 Moon Sign Pisces

There is certainly more than one way to get ahead. With a wealth of new projects about to be launched, the only real problem now is finding enough time to get everything done. This difficulty can be addressed by getting other people involved from the start.

20 FRIDAY
Moon Age Day 0 Moon Sign Pisces

If you spend too much time thinking about the future today, you get very little done in the present. It is vital to keep your eye firmly on the ball in some situations, at least. When it comes to having fun, you won't discover many obstacles at all. Simply find a friend and pitch in.

21 SATURDAY
Moon Age Day 1 Moon Sign Aries

You are clearly very anxious to push ahead at the moment, though any real progress can be delayed this weekend, mainly because there are ways to have fun that you will not wish to miss. There is a distinct possibility that you will get the urge to travel now, if not to exotic places, then at least to profitable ones.

22 SUNDAY
Moon Age Day 2 Moon Sign Aries

Some of the ways you choose to solve personal problems are unique, to say the least. It might be suggested that you are somewhat unrealistic at the moment, though you would doubtless disagree. In the end, you are more or less forced to do things your own way. You can't help it; it's called being a Leo.

23 MONDAY
Moon Age Day 3 Moon Sign Taurus

Today you have the ability to charm those higher up the ladder of life to give you a hand up. Some Leo people will be offered additional responsibilities at this time and are unlikely to turn down the opportunity. Conforming to expectations in a social sense isn't easy, but people are relying on you.

24 TUESDAY
Moon Age Day 4 Moon Sign Taurus

This is a time for getting down to the real nitty-gritty of situations and for thinking them through very carefully indeed. Some conflict amongst your friends can be solved in minutes with your timely intervention, whilst romance looks better and stronger than for some days past.

Your Daily Guide to March 2015

25 WEDNESDAY
Moon Age Day 5 Moon Sign Gemini

You seem to know instinctively today which elements of life you need to retain and which should be jettisoned. You are not in the least sentimental right now and would be quite willing to shove all manner of things in the dustbin. This doesn't simply include old furnishings, but a few redundant thoughts, too.

26 THURSDAY
Moon Age Day 6 Moon Sign Gemini

Now is the time for genuinely assessing what is going on in your life and making a few minor alterations, especially with regard to professional matters. There is the possibility of meeting people from the past, some of whom could have a fairly important part to play in your thinking for the future.

27 FRIDAY
Moon Age Day 7 Moon Sign Cancer

Personal freedom is likely to be emphasised above everything right now. This is fine in principle, but you might take things too far. Try to relax more and to accept the benefits that today offers. If you are obliged to work, don't do any more than is strictly necessary.

28 SATURDAY
Moon Age Day 8 Moon Sign Cancer

Getting on with others might not be too easy. If you want to make certain that there are no hiccups in relationships today, you need to stay close to those individuals who know you well and who are invariably on your side. You may begin to question some aspects of your social circle around now.

29 SUNDAY
Moon Age Day 9 Moon Sign Cancer

You could find yourself in the right place at the best time to make a financial killing of some sort. This situation could easily be linked with medium and long-term planning from the past, which is finally maturing. Don't be too ready to judge the actions of a friend without checking matters with them.

30 MONDAY
Moon Age Day 10 Moon Sign Leo

Now is the time to get your foot down on the professional accelerator. You know what you want from life, and have a pretty good idea how you should go about getting it. There are details today that must not be left to chance and you cannot assume that they will sort themselves out.

Your Daily Guide to March 2015

31 TUESDAY
Moon Age Day 11   Moon Sign Leo

Both mental and physical strengths are much emphasised. It appears that you are now filled with optimism, and for this reason alone you can get on well. Don't be too quick to make broad-based changes, but do move forward progressively with specific plans.

2015

YOUR MONTH AT A GLANCE

⊕ = Opportunities are around ⊖ = Be on the defensive = Life is pretty ordinary

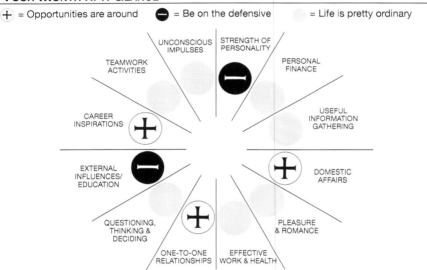

APRIL HIGHS AND LOWS

Here I show you how the rhythms of the Moon will affect you this month. Like the tide, your energies and abilities will rise and fall with its pattern. When it is above the centre line, go for it, when it is below, you should be resting.

HIGH 26TH–28TH

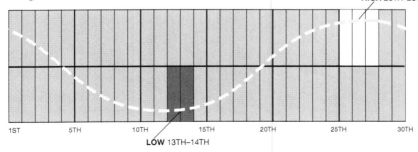

LOW 13TH–14TH

Your Daily Guide to April 2015

1 WEDNESDAY
Moon Age Day 12   Moon Sign Virgo

Jumping about from one foot to another is not typical of your zodiac sign, but that is the way things will be for the moment. You give others the wrong impression if you are indecisive, so it might be best to avoid making decisions at all, unless circumstances force you to do so. Keep a sense of proportion.

2 THURSDAY
Moon Age Day 13   Moon Sign Virgo

Try to vary your routines as much as possible today. It is easy for you to become bored at present, so do what you can to keep things fresh. The social side of life appeals to you the most and offers you the chance to bring change and diversity into your life. Plan now for an active and enterprising weekend.

3 FRIDAY
Moon Age Day 14   Moon Sign Virgo

The time is right for communication, so keep an eye out for social offers coming in from a number of different directions. What you are enjoying the most at the moment is popularity, and there's nothing that suits your zodiac sign right now more than that.

4 SATURDAY
Moon Age Day 15   Moon Sign Libra

Whatever you do makes a great different this weekend. You don't have to move mountains to let others know you are around. Your general state of mind is positive and you are now constantly thinking up new ways to get ahead. Saturday brings you many chances to have fun, so you won't have to take life too seriously.

5 SUNDAY
Moon Age Day 16   Moon Sign Libra

The tempo of everyday life is fast and furious. Keeping abreast of all possible situations isn't going to be easy, but if anyone is equal to this task it's you. Conversations of all kinds can pay significant dividends – that is, if you don't allow a temporary Leo argumentative streak to show itself too much.

6 MONDAY
Moon Age Day 17   Moon Sign Scorpio

Although you are generally on a roll at the moment, you shouldn't take everything you hear at face value. There is evidence that if there is one day of the month on which you could easily be duped, that day is here. In your dealings with the world at large, you will want to give good value for money, even if you have to put yourself out.

Your Daily Guide to April 2015

7 TUESDAY
Moon Age Day 18 Moon Sign Scorpio

Financially speaking this could be quite a trying period, which is why you have to keep a close eye on where the pennies are going. Avoid lavish expenditure in any direction; if possible, spend little or nothing for the moment. It could be difficult to tell when people are trying to take you for a ride.

8 WEDNESDAY
Moon Age Day 19 Moon Sign Scorpio

Along comes a day when it ought to be more than possible to do your own thing. You won't take kindly to being told what to do, or how to go about it. Leo can be quite touchy at the moment and there are occasions when it really would make sense to bite your tongue. There is a danger of spoiling your own business later if you are not careful.

9 THURSDAY
Moon Age Day 20 Moon Sign Sagittarius

You show a ready wit and a tendency to fire back quickly today, though without any venom and in ways that will make others laugh. At heart, you are a real old softy and ought to be more than willing to help out whenever you can. Charity work of almost any sort might begin to appeal to you around this time.

10 FRIDAY
Moon Age Day 21 Moon Sign Sagittarius

Don't expect everyone to agree with your ideas at present. There are people around whose opinions are radically different from yours and there is little chance of you getting your own way in the end. The more conciliatory you are, the more likely you will be to make unexpected gains, and a few new friends on the way.

11 SATURDAY
Moon Age Day 22 Moon Sign Capricorn

This is an ideal time for socialising and you are more than willing to rub shoulders with people who are new to your life. There is a distinct possibility that you could be making friends who will stay around in your life for a long time to come. Good pals are hard to come by, so keep your eyes open.

12 SUNDAY
Moon Age Day 23 Moon Sign Capricorn

This is a time when you can get things organised and during which you are clearly in the market for a challenge. Although Sunday might make social demands, you are still able to look practical matters squarely in the face. Hard work is something that doesn't frighten you in the least, as you are about to discover.

Your Daily Guide to April 2015

13 MONDAY
Moon Age Day 24 Moon Sign Aquarius

Even though there is a lunar low, new input could come your way. Whatever else you do, keep your ears open. Under current trends, there could be gains for the taking at work, with colleagues and superiors alike more than willing to lend a hand. Leo is in for good times, but just make sure you don't look any sort of gift horse in the mouth.

14 TUESDAY
Moon Age Day 25 Moon Sign Aquarius

There are minor setbacks today, particularly in a career sense, and there isn't really a great deal you can do about the situation except to be patient. The lunar low will be out of the way tomorrow and then you can concentrate once again on getting ahead. Confidence to do the right thing ought to stay generally high.

15 WEDNESDAY
Moon Age Day 26 Moon Sign Pisces

Ingenuity is now the way to success. Don't take anything at face value and if some of your original ideas are being shunned, it's up to you to explain yourself over again. Don't take no for an answer, especially on those occasions when you know full well you are right in what you are saying. Creative potential looks good.

16 THURSDAY
Moon Age Day 27 Moon Sign Pisces

Keep your ideas today as interesting and varied as possible. You can do without taking on any extra responsibilities, because you need to spend some time on yourself for once. Romance looks good, with a possible highpoint arriving around now.

17 FRIDAY
Moon Age Day 28 Moon Sign Aries

There can be very fruitful forms of co-operation with a number of different people at the moment. On a business front you may now be having new ideas that are both inspirational and fun, whilst you are also likely to be experience some unexpected popularity when in social situations.

18 SATURDAY
Moon Age Day 29 Moon Sign Aries

This is a time for pleasantries, particularly where your general social life is concerned. Leo people who are not involved in a permanent romantic attachment should keep their eyes open, and all Lions can expect a greater than average share of positive attention from the world at large.

Your Daily Guide to April 2015

19 SUNDAY
Moon Age Day 0   Moon Sign Taurus

Find something that you can accomplish today and get cracking just as hard as you can. This is not likely to be a particularly restful Sunday, but it ought to be very interesting. Social outings, either during the day or in the evening, leave you feeling quite contented and happy with your lot.

20 MONDAY
Moon Age Day 1   Moon Sign Taurus

Group situations are well starred, and there appears to be a good deal to keep you happy at present. You may be getting somewhat tired of certain routines, and probably feel you need a rest. The stars cannot promise that, but what they do indicate is a gradual but radical change of emphasis, which is nearly as good.

21 TUESDAY
Moon Age Day 2   Moon Sign Gemini

There could be help available where professional developments are concerned. It would be sensible today to listen to the advice of people who are real professionals in their respective fields. After all, it isn't possible to be good at absolutely everything, even though Leo tries to make it so.

22 WEDNESDAY
Moon Age Day 3   Moon Sign Gemini

A boost to your career prospects is on the cards. People are more than happy to put you in charge of situations, both inside work and out. Socially speaking, not everyone is going to prove to be your cup of tea today, and it could prove hard to stay away from the individuals who are not.

23 THURSDAY
Moon Age Day 4   Moon Sign Gemini

Certain professional moves you are making at the moment ought to leave you feeling quite delighted with the results. Your suspicions may be aroused regarding the actions of family members and if so you will want to offer a degree of support. Meanwhile, you get the opportunity to please yourself more over domestic issues.

24 FRIDAY
Moon Age Day 5   Moon Sign Cancer

Only you can decide whether to rely on what you hear at work this Friday. In this sphere of your life, and possibly even in others, you can be badly misled. It's a case of using a mixture of common sense and intuition, in order to avoid a few complications cropping up later.

Your Daily Guide to April 2015

25 SATURDAY
Moon Age Day 6 Moon Sign Cancer

You can afford to open your mind to the outside world and stimulate those little grey cells this Saturday. Your attitude is one of optimism, tinged with a sense of reality that not everyone in your vicinity is showing right now. Conforming to expectations in social situations might be boring, so don't bother.

26 SUNDAY
Moon Age Day 7 Moon Sign Leo

The remainder of the weekend ought to be bright, breezy and full of fun. The lunar high offers vitality and the ability to keep going, even when others are dropping from exhaustion. You are fighting fit and anxious to do anything possible to increase your experience of life. Surely this is the zodiac sign of Leo working at its best.

27 MONDAY
Moon Age Day 8 Moon Sign Leo

It's hard to put a foot wrong today. People like you, and are quite willing to show it on almost any occasion. Although you won't be stopped when you have made up your mind to any specific course of action, you need to allow others to do things on your behalf. Tedious jobs around the home won't be relished now.

28 TUESDAY
Moon Age Day 9 Moon Sign Leo

The time is right for spending quality time with your partner or maybe even members of the family. It is true that you may not be quite as busy in a work or practical sense as is sometimes the case. However, everyone needs a break, even the average Leo.

29 WEDNESDAY
Moon Age Day 10 Moon Sign Virgo

There are signs that there could be some emotional disappointments to be dealt with today, especially regarding your love life. These can be dealt with fairly easily, just as long as you are willing to talk things through. An understanding attitude on your part also assists in curing an ill that goes back quite some time.

30 THURSDAY
Moon Age Day 11 Moon Sign Virgo

There could be the odd financial hiccup today, which will need dealing with before you move onwards in your life. Although this is not the sort of period when you are worrying about situations too much, you might be slightly inclined to fret over family issues, most of which will resolve themselves, given time.

May 2015

Your Month at a Glance

+ = Opportunities are around   ● = Be on the defensive   = Life is pretty ordinary

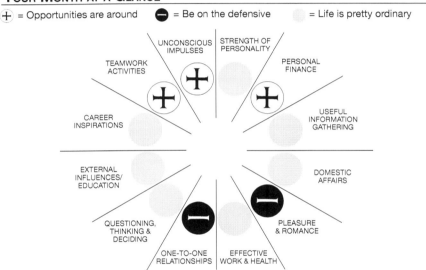

May Highs and Lows

Here I show you how the rhythms of the Moon will affect you this month. Like the tide, your energies and abilities will rise and fall with its pattern. When it is above the centre line, go for it, when it is below, you should be resting.

HIGH 23RD–25TH

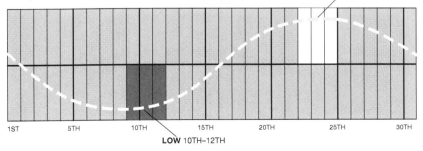

LOW 10TH–12TH

Your Daily Guide to May 2015

1 FRIDAY
Moon Age Day 12 Moon Sign Libra

Getting along with others certainly does not have to be a battle today, but you tend to see it as such on too many occasions. Listen carefully to what is being said to you, and keep your opinions on hold until you have done so. In the end, you may well realise that your opinions are broadly the same as those of other people.

2 SATURDAY
Moon Age Day 13 Moon Sign Libra

Happiness to you at the moment is likely to mean being on the move. An early holiday would suit you just fine, but if this isn't possible at least try to vary your routines as much as possible. Avoid staying in the same place for too long and make sure that variety also represents a strong element of your social life.

3 SUNDAY
Moon Age Day 14 Moon Sign Libra

Today's influences indicate that this would be a wonderful time for getting on the right side of your boss. A shame, then, that so few Leo people will actually be at work today. Nevertheless, you can at least influence others positively in your social and family life. Everything comes together to make you charming, yet incisive and determined.

4 MONDAY
Moon Age Day 15 Moon Sign Scorpio

Friendships and group encounters take on a particularly pleasant feel right now. Confidence is still present, and this is the component of nature that makes the difference between a happy and a miserable Leo subject. Creative potential around now means you might think about changes regarding your home.

5 TUESDAY
Moon Age Day 16 Moon Sign Scorpio

Financial matters should be looking stronger as the day goes on. Although you may be in a position to gamble a little, some circumspection is necessary at first. New ideas could be coming to you at any time now and you will probably be willing to listen to the advice of good friends. You will want to be active in your social life.

6 WEDNESDAY
Moon Age Day 17 Moon Sign Sagittarius

Some information you receive today could turn out to be very valuable. There are enlightening times ahead and perhaps a meeting with people who are going to be of great value in your life eventually. Existing pals want to spend time with you, but there are choices to be made at a time when you are so busy.

Your Daily Guide to May 2015

7 THURSDAY
Moon Age Day 18 Moon Sign Sagittarius

Communication is well marked today, and there is information coming your way at any time now that could prove to be extremely useful. On the personal front, relationships are looking especially good and there could not be a better time than this for speaking words of love to someone who is extra special. The kinder and gentler side of your nature is now on display.

8 FRIDAY
Moon Age Day 19 Moon Sign Capricorn

It takes a good deal of courage to admit that you might have been wrong. If you have to eat a little humble pie at some stage today, make sure you do so with a good heart. It would be better to say nothing, rather than grudgingly to admit anything at all. Those who know you well have some words of wisdom later.

9 SATURDAY
Moon Age Day 20 Moon Sign Capricorn

Your strength lies in your considerable charm right now. Almost anyone you come across will notice this and that means a boost to your personal popularity. Look after money carefully, particularly later in the day, when you may be faced with a bargain that looks just too good.

10 SUNDAY
Moon Age Day 21 Moon Sign Aquarius

How much you actually achieve today is really dependent on the way you approach life. You have to remember that the lunar low is around at the moment, so pushing yourself too hard really won't help very much. Concentrate on the task in hand and deliberately steer clear of stress.

11 MONDAY
Moon Age Day 22 Moon Sign Aquarius

Ordinary progress is possible today, but anything beyond that is likely to be rather difficult. Once the lunar low is out of the way, you will move forwards progressively, but in the meantime you will have to make do with second best. Remain social and spend as much time as possible with relatives and good friends.

12 TUESDAY
Moon Age Day 23 Moon Sign Aquarius

Under present influences, today offers you the chance to come good on promises you have made previously, and in particular much positive action is directed towards house and home. Keep an open mind about proffered changes on the work front and don't dismiss offers of new responsibilities.

Your Daily Guide to May 2015

13 WEDNESDAY
Moon Age Day 24 Moon Sign Pisces

Spirits might not be quite as high as you would like, but that doesn't mean you are particularly slowing down. It may be that you simply don't have quite your usual level of self-confidence, though this situation will change soon enough. By the evening, you will probably be in the right frame of mind to party.

14 THURSDAY
Moon Age Day 25 Moon Sign Pisces

Input and information relating to present schemes and plans are important to you this Thursday. It does no harm to dream, especially about things that stand a good chance of becoming a reality in the fullness of time. A practical approach to personal situations finds you breaking new ground and explaining yourself wonderfully.

15 FRIDAY
Moon Age Day 26 Moon Sign Aries

Beware that co-operative affairs could be slightly marred by arguments this Friday. Most of these are not at all necessary and it would be far better not to allow yourself to become too involved. If you can't avoid being in contentious situations, use the full force of your persuasive nature to draw a line under potential problems.

16 SATURDAY
Moon Age Day 27 Moon Sign Aries

This would be a good time to make sure you have your eyes and ears open because there is a good deal of fresh input coming along today. You might also feel the need of some fresh air and certainly will not take kindly to being cooped up all day long. A certain restless streak begins to develop.

17 SUNDAY
Moon Age Day 28 Moon Sign Taurus

Enjoying all that domestic relationships have to offer you could prove somewhat more difficult today. Don't be surprised if you don't get on with everyone at home right now. It will seem from your point of view that someone is being distinctly difficult, but it is possible you should be looking in the mirror.

18 MONDAY
Moon Age Day 0 Moon Sign Taurus

The emphasis today is on the wider social world and it is just possible that your work will take something of a back seat. You probably have a few inspirational ideas in your head and will want to get a few of them moving in the real world. You could do better than to look for some support right now.

Your Daily Guide to May 2015

19 TUESDAY ☿ *Moon Age Day 1 Moon Sign Gemini*

The chances of success in professional matters are high today. Almost immediately you pick up the traces of issues that were important to you in the not too distant past. Chasing details is a piece of cake and it is very unlikely that anyone could fool you in any way at present.

20 WEDNESDAY ☿ *Moon Age Day 2 Moon Sign Gemini*

This is a good time to broaden your intellectual and social interests. Pleasure trips are indicated and you could discover that cultural interests are enhanced. Leo people who are not at work today will be the luckiest, making this a good candidate for a day off, if you can swing it.

21 THURSDAY ☿ *Moon Age Day 3 Moon Sign Cancer*

You need to treat this day with some respect. It won't help if you insist on doing practical things or even domestic chores to the extent that you drive yourself mad with them. What really works today is some diversity and a little excitement. You have strong enough powers of persuasion to get others to join in.

22 FRIDAY ☿ *Moon Age Day 4 Moon Sign Cancer*

Maximise your potential today by being a true Leo. You can afford to be bold and fearless, partly because you retain another Leo quality: a sense of honour. You won't do anything that materially or personally works against the best interests of others. Like the regal creature you are, you watch over your subjects.

23 SATURDAY ☿ *Moon Age Day 5 Moon Sign Leo*

Saturday brings positive aspects to bear on you. With plenty of energy and a great desire to get on, you could get through a breathtaking amount. Avoid family arguments and stay out there in the mainstream of life. That is where you will feel most comfortable and the place you make the greatest impression.

24 SUNDAY ☿ *Moon Age Day 6 Moon Sign Leo*

Sunday shows a continuation of the generally favourable trends that surround you at present. Although there is plenty to be done, you approach all jobs with a cheerful attitude. If there is a need in your life at the moment to tell others how they should behave, this might be a good day to speak out.

Your Daily Guide to May 2015

25 MONDAY ☿ *Moon Age Day 7 Moon Sign Leo*

You are unlikely to be thwarted today, once you have made up your mind to a particular course of action. You know what you want from life and have a very good idea how to get it. Your typical Leo traits are definitely in evidence, and continue to be so for the whole of the day and beyond.

26 TUESDAY ☿ *Moon Age Day 8 Moon Sign Virgo*

There is a warning today that you could end up in an undesirable situation if you put trust in the wrong people, so it is vital that you take nothing at all for granted. Rather, you should be more cautious than usual and ensure that you ask the most searching of questions, especially regarding contracts.

27 WEDNESDAY ☿ *Moon Age Day 9 Moon Sign Virgo*

Take advantage of the planetary trends highlighting work and financial developments generally. Make sure you don't push your nervous system too hard, because, like everyone else in the world, you can go too far. It's hard to believe that fact at the moment, but if you don't take some rest you will discover the truth of the matter.

28 THURSDAY ☿ *Moon Age Day 10 Moon Sign Libra*

This is likely to be a very busy day. Negotiations and communications generally are the area of life that interests you specifically and you won't take too kindly to anyone who appears to throw a spanner in the works. You should find time to entertain family members and to make a fuss of your partner.

29 FRIDAY ☿ *Moon Age Day 11 Moon Sign Libra*

The contacts you have with others are lively and rewarding. Committing yourself exclusively to business is not something that is likely to appeal all that much. You are clear in your mind that you need alternatives to the cut and thrust of your practical life. Capturing your own interest with a new stimulus is not difficult.

30 SATURDAY ☿ *Moon Age Day 12 Moon Sign Libra*

There are definite patterns to life, some of which you fail to recognise in the cut and thrust of everyday life. These patterns show all the more because you are somewhat more contemplative at present. For the next few days, think deeply and you could reach some very important conclusions.

Your Daily Guide to May 2015

31 SUNDAY   ☿

Moon Age Day 13 Moon Sign Scorpio

You will have little patience with mundane tasks today, so your best interests could be served by spending at least part of the weekend doing exactly what takes your fancy. There is no problem with this way of thinking, just as long as the really essential tasks are taken care of before you start galloping off in different directions.

  2015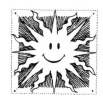

Your Month at a Glance

⊕ = Opportunities are around   ⊖ = Be on the defensive   ○ = Life is pretty ordinary

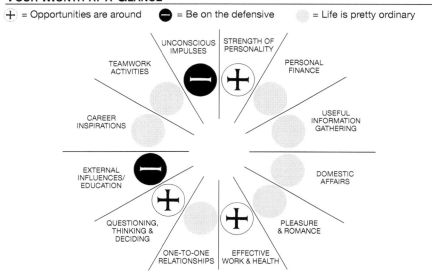

June Highs and Lows

Here I show you how the rhythms of the Moon will affect you this month. Like the tide, your energies and abilities will rise and fall with its pattern. When it is above the centre line, go for it, when it is below, you should be resting.

HIGH 20TH–21ST

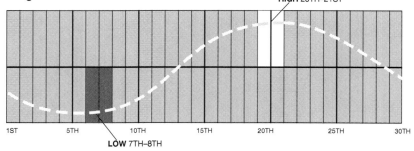

LOW 7TH–8TH

Your Daily Guide to June 2015

1 MONDAY ☿ *Moon Age Day 14 Moon Sign Scorpio*

There are high points in your social and domestic life that compensate for a slightly lacklustre time at work. Romance is worth a second look, especially if you are without a partner at present. If you keep your eyes open, you will realise that there are people around who find you very attractive.

2 TUESDAY ☿ *Moon Age Day 15 Moon Sign Sagittarius*

This is likely to be a very demanding period on the domestic front. Although there is plenty to keep you busy at work, people at home are also definitely seeking your attention. Split your time as best you can, but avoid crowding your schedule. If necessary, leave practical matters until later.

3 WEDNESDAY ☿ *Moon Age Day 16 Moon Sign Sagittarius*

A genuine love of life ought to be enhanced at the moment as a result of gatherings and meetings with some fairly influential people. You may have to do some serious thinking today, but this is hardly likely to have any bearing at all on the personal or social aspects of life. Leave one or two major jobs until tomorrow.

4 THURSDAY ☿ *Moon Age Day 17 Moon Sign Sagittarius*

There is a possibility that you will be feeling too emotional today. If this does turn out to be the case, you could also register waves of nostalgia washing over you. Leo is certainly not immune from looking back sometimes; it's simply part of the mechanism that tunes your sensibilities for the future.

5 FRIDAY ☿ *Moon Age Day 18 Moon Sign Capricorn*

Initiating new ideas can be very productive now, both for medium and long-term objectives. Share some of your schemes with people who are in the know and avoid keeping things to yourself that are totally dependent on co-operation. An over-suspicious attitude now is only going to hold you back later.

6 SATURDAY ☿ *Moon Age Day 19 Moon Sign Capricorn*

Don't be surprised if you discover this weekend that over-optimism can be something of a drawback. You need to be circumspect, but without coming across as too suspicious. With the warmer summer weather now beginning to show itself, you may be keen to get out and about, and maybe even planning a holiday before long.

Your Daily Guide to June 2015

7 SUNDAY ☿ *Moon Age Day 20 Moon Sign Aquarius*

Vitality is likely to be in short supply today, for which you can blame the lunar low. You just don't have the drive and enthusiasm that often accompanies your life and will have to make excuses for the fact. Judge today and tomorrow as an interlude designed for thinking.

8 MONDAY ☿ *Moon Age Day 21 Moon Sign Aquarius*

Don't be too concerned with the future, except in terms of looking ahead in your mind and sorting out minor details. There will probably be a quiet start to the week, but that doesn't mean to say you will want to be stuck indoors. The time could be right for looking at the needs of your partner.

9 TUESDAY ☿ *Moon Age Day 22 Moon Sign Pisces*

This is a day when you tend to think the best of other people. It's a strange fact of life, but when you behave in that way people will invariably come good on their promises. Optimism rides high in Leo and you have the ability to move minor mountains when you experience this frame of mind.

10 WEDNESDAY ☿ *Moon Age Day 23 Moon Sign Pisces*

Today you find that a desire for freedom, together with the chance to do your own thing, proves to be very important. You may still be slightly tied down by a sense of responsibility, but there are ways and means of lightening the load. Try to float through situations that on some occasions have the power to make you hopping mad.

11 THURSDAY ☿ *Moon Age Day 24 Moon Sign Aries*

False modesty is something of a waste of time as far as you are concerned. People can see through it easily and it simply doesn't suit the sort of person you are. Strangely enough, you may be nervous about something you are going to undertake soon, though you would do almost anything to hide the fact from the world at large.

12 FRIDAY ☿ *Moon Age Day 25 Moon Sign Aries*

This would be an especially good time for group encounters, so sticking to just one individual doesn't suit you particularly well right now. There could be a conflict here, because someone who is especially close to you needs constant reassurance. Walking this tightrope isn't easy, but it can be achieved with concentration.

Your Daily Guide to June 2015

13 SATURDAY
Moon Age Day 26   Moon Sign Taurus

You are going to great lengths to please other people, but don't be surprised if you fail to make everyone happy. At the end of the day, you have to decide what you know to be best for everyone concerned and to act accordingly. Those who disagree with you at first should soon come round.

14 SUNDAY
Moon Age Day 27   Moon Sign Taurus

There may be a practical setback. If this has anything to do with house and home, it could be better to leave others to sort things out. Treat yourself in some way today, by getting out of the house and maybe with a journey. You still need change and diversity, together with good social potential.

15 MONDAY
Moon Age Day 28   Moon Sign Gemini

It is possible that there will be niggles at home caused by people who have agendas that are not the same as yours. Avoid tension by refusing to get involved in disputes that are not of your making. Indeed, you could find yourself in the position of being an honest broker when others cannot see eye to eye.

16 TUESDAY
Moon Age Day 29   Moon Sign Gemini

Some distractions are likely today, particularly when it comes to your professional life. This Tuesday almost certainly promises entertainment, much of which is inspired by your own efforts. New friends are there for the taking at this time and you would be somewhat foolish to ignore the fact.

17 WEDNESDAY
Moon Age Day 0   Moon Sign Cancer

It's good to be out there amongst peer groups, steering the course of the future, not only for yourself but also for them. People expect you to take a leading role in a number of different projects and you may also be thinking some up for yourself. Leo is particularly innovative at this time.

18 THURSDAY
Moon Age Day 1   Moon Sign Cancer

The time is right for addressing tensions. If you find yourself absolutely forced into taking a specific point of view, do so without any doubt in your mind. Most people, especially family members, will be happy to opt for a good time, which it is within your power to offer.

Your Daily Guide to June 2015

19 FRIDAY
Moon Age Day 2 Moon Sign Cancer

Friends and friendships are favoured today. Your powers of attraction are strong and will continue to be so for some days to come. On the romantic front, you are more or less automatically saying the sort of things that your lover will find immensely attractive and very flattering.

20 SATURDAY
Moon Age Day 3 Moon Sign Leo

During this period you are able to steam ahead, even if the fact that the weekend is here slows the more professional aspirations somewhat. This should be a good day for shopping and for acquiring something you have been wanting for a while. Although there is a lot of work ahead of you, the prospects are especially good.

21 SUNDAY
Moon Age Day 4 Moon Sign Leo

You are in a position to talk almost anyone into anything at the moment, though you will almost certainly restrict yourself to individuals who seem to have been taking a somewhat shaky path of late. In addition, you are funny and very resourceful. Altogether, this is a winning combination for the end of this particular week.

22 MONDAY
Moon Age Day 5 Moon Sign Virgo

Today's sources of joy and pleasure should be friends and colleagues, most of whom are doing what they can to be supportive of your ideas and plans. This isn't exclusively the case, but there is no reason whatsoever today to defend yourself before you are attacked in any way.

23 TUESDAY
Moon Age Day 6 Moon Sign Virgo

Prepare to make the most of your active imagination, which could be working overtime at the moment. This might lead you to contemplate some rather unlikely and possibly even potentially troubling scenarios, but it also offers you a sort of genius for the future that is more than useful.

24 WEDNESDAY
Moon Age Day 7 Moon Sign Virgo

All sorts of social interactions seem heaven sent at present. You have the means to improve communications between yourself and others, as well as extra incentive to travel to particularly interesting places. In any given situation, it is now better to reserve your judgement, rather than to act on impulse.

Your Daily Guide to June 2015

25 THURSDAY
Moon Age Day 8 Moon Sign Libra

Don't let the planetary trends stop you from thinking clearly. Be willing to seek out the impartial advice of good friends, or people who are experts in their own given fields. After all, you can't be excellent at everything, even if you would wish to be.

26 FRIDAY
Moon Age Day 9 Moon Sign Libra

Some of your more grandiose expectations will have to be played down today, or there could be some disappointments on the way. Simply remain realistic in your approach to life and don't be too willing to take a point of view that others would see as being both radical and probably unworkable.

27 SATURDAY
Moon Age Day 10 Moon Sign Scorpio

There is no need at all to assume that things are going wrong, simply because life might be rather quiet at the beginning of the weekend. It is really up to you to add the events and the incentives today. This would be an excellent time for a shopping spree, with some bargains in the offing.

28 SUNDAY
Moon Age Day 11 Moon Sign Scorpio

Today is best served by taking life steadily. There is nothing to be gained at present from pushing yourself too hard and a contemplative approach to most situations will work out best. Finances might respond to a special overview, but don't take any drastic action.

29 MONDAY
Moon Age Day 12 Moon Sign Scorpio

Opt for some light relief if at all possible, because this is not the day on which you ought to take yourself or anyone else too seriously. In a social sense you can lighten the load of a number of different individuals, as well as taking the sting out of a situation that could otherwise lead to unnecessary arguments.

30 TUESDAY
Moon Age Day 13 Moon Sign Sagittarius

There could be scope for some shortcuts to better prospects, particularly in terms of family finances. This is not the only matter on your mind, however, because much of today is about having a good time. The most important fact to remember at present is not to take yourself or anyone else too seriously.

July 2015

Your Month at a Glance

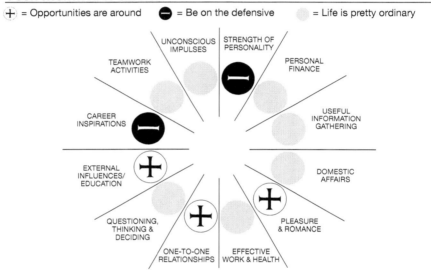

⊕ = Opportunities are around   ⊖ = Be on the defensive   ○ = Life is pretty ordinary

July Highs and Lows

Here I show you how the rhythms of the Moon will affect you this month. Like the tide, your energies and abilities will rise and fall with its pattern. When it is above the centre line, go for it, when it is below, you should be resting.

HIGH 17TH–19TH

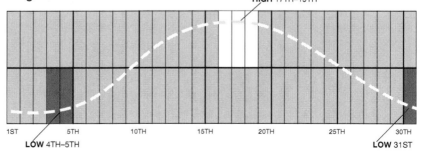

LOW 4TH–5TH   **LOW** 31ST

Your Daily Guide to July 2015

1 WEDNESDAY *Moon Age Day 14 Moon Sign Sagittarius*

A new romantic high-spot comes along, which allows you to make your deepest emotions known, even if the recipient is not even party to your feelings yet. As the saying goes: 'Faint heart never won fair lady', or handsome man for that matter. Maybe it's time to speak out, even if you fear a rebuff.

2 THURSDAY *Moon Age Day 15 Moon Sign Capricorn*

Domestic issues put a smile on your face, thanks to the position of the Sun in your solar chart. Keep an open mind about intended changes at work and don't be put off by people who clearly have no idea what they are talking about. A few interruptions are inevitable, but they probably won't be too disruptive.

3 FRIDAY *Moon Age Day 16 Moon Sign Capricorn*

Your strength lies in your attitude to life and the people you meet, and there are pleasant times to be had today. With a cheerful smile, you are able to counter any criticism that comes your way and you should discover that your general popularity is definitely on the increase.

4 SATURDAY *Moon Age Day 17 Moon Sign Aquarius*

Communication issues are on your mind, as the whole world and his dog seem to want to talk to you right now. There are a few people around who want to change your opinions, but there isn't really very much chance of that happening. Look out for the chance to embark on a new adventure before very long.

5 SUNDAY *Moon Age Day 18 Moon Sign Aquarius*

Though you remain generally optimistic, not everyone around you enjoys the same level of confidence. As a result, you will have to spend at least part of today convincing others that you know what you are talking about. Hang on in there, even if the going gets tough. There are gains for Leo people with staying power.

6 MONDAY *Moon Age Day 19 Moon Sign Pisces*

It is the small things of life that ought to be addressed today. Probably just as well, because you are not exactly in the mood to take on anything major. Social functions ought to appeal and there will be the chance to get out into the fresh air. Family parties or informal functions could also be fun.

Your Daily Guide to July 2015

7 TUESDAY
Moon Age Day 20 Moon Sign Pisces

You might not be entirely responsible if you are in a state of disorganisation today, but there is a chance you are contributing to it. Try to stay cool, calm and collected, even if you feel there is some provocation about. In particular, it would be most sensible to avoid becoming involved in family disputes.

8 WEDNESDAY
Moon Age Day 21 Moon Sign Aries

You can get just as much from listening to others today as you can from contributing to situations yourself. In a practical sense, you will now want to be ahead of the game and you could also discover a sporting attitude developing inside you. Try to vary life and take what you can from positive prevailing circumstances in love matches.

9 THURSDAY
Moon Age Day 22 Moon Sign Aries

What you learn today could be of tremendous importance in the longer term, which is why it is important to pay attention to what is being said in your immediate vicinity. There is a possibility of new love interests coming into the lives of available Leo subjects, together with a strengthening of ties for most.

10 FRIDAY
Moon Age Day 23 Moon Sign Taurus

The time is right for romance. You enjoy being number one and that is the position that you are inclined to occupy in the mind of a number of people right now. Even so, you cannot be everyone's cup of tea. You will have to accept this, albeit reluctantly.

11 SATURDAY
Moon Age Day 24 Moon Sign Taurus

Since work matters tend to be progressive and more or less looking after themselves, you are left to consider social and personal matters instead. The response you give to offers that are coming your way at this time is going to be quite important. Energy and determination appear to be going hand in hand for the moment.

12 SUNDAY
Moon Age Day 25 Moon Sign Taurus

You are likely to be happiest at home today. There are some minor frustrations about, but you tend to deal with these quickly and efficiently. If you find you have something to tackle that you really don't want to do, it might be best to face it very early in the day. At least that way there will be more moments to please yourself later.

Your Daily Guide to July 2015

13 MONDAY
Moon Age Day 26   Moon Sign Gemini

Focus on love life and romance as this new week begins. There is a good deal of ego fulfilment in the offing and so you notice that your popularity is particularly high. Making the right sort of decision should be easy, especially if you are willing to listen to the well-intentioned and quite sensible advice of friends.

14 TUESDAY
Moon Age Day 27   Moon Sign Gemini

Someone, somewhere will almost certainly be making you feel good today. It's the little things in life that please you the most and that offer you the best chance to feel good about yourself. The kind side of your Leo nature is quite definitely on display and it is likely to remain so for the next couple of days and beyond.

15 WEDNESDAY
Moon Age Day 28   Moon Sign Cancer

Your personality now has a strong impact on the world at large and especially on people who have been watching you closely for some time. Keep up your efforts to get on well at work and don't turn down the chance of some extra responsibilities, simply because you have doubts about your abilities.

16 THURSDAY
Moon Age Day 0   Moon Sign Cancer

Prepare to make the most of time spent on your own today and it will not be wasted. The Moon in your solar twelfth house often leads to a more contemplative attitude and a greater desire to think things through. Although this fact could appear to make you rather less social than of late, those around you could be too busy to notice the fact.

17 FRIDAY
Moon Age Day 1   Moon Sign Leo

Personal and professional objectives are worth chasing today, with the lunar high giving you staying power and a desire to get ahead. Confidence is especially high and once again you could be turning your mind to love. For at least a few Leo subjects, this is the time for popping an important question.

18 SATURDAY
Moon Age Day 2   Moon Sign Leo

Your judgement in major decisions seems to be especially good right now and that is why you are able to take a chance or two that under normal circumstances you might not. Entertaining, bright, happy and charming, there is no doubt that you have the ability to turn a few heads, particularly in social outings tonight.

Your Daily Guide to July 2015

19 SUNDAY
Moon Age Day 3 Moon Sign Leo

You may well encounter a few obstacles today, which won't go down too well after two days when it seemed as though you were monarch of the world. Don't get too carried away by big ideas and try to be modest in your expectations. True, this isn't going to be easy, but it does pay the best dividends in the end.

20 MONDAY
Moon Age Day 4 Moon Sign Virgo

You tend to be bolder than ever at present and will be quite keen to take a few chances. That is fine, just as long as the risks are calculated carefully. Where you should avoid them altogether is with regard to money. If you have documents to sign, read the small print carefully.

21 TUESDAY
Moon Age Day 5 Moon Sign Virgo

You will want to be on the move today and so will not take kindly to any situation that ties you exclusively to a particular spot. Give yourself a pat on the back for recent successes at work, but do not allow these to go to your head. There is still plenty to do if you want to get exactly where you need to be.

22 WEDNESDAY
Moon Age Day 6 Moon Sign Libra

You are likely to enjoy being on the go from morning 'til night this Wednesday, though you would gain by staying away from situations that mean working in the strict sense of the word. What is needed most of all is enjoyment. As long as this is present, you can do almost anything.

23 THURSDAY
Moon Age Day 7 Moon Sign Libra

Socially speaking, your powers of attraction are strong and you are inclined to seek out likeminded people at the moment. Don't be in the least surprised if you are being fancied by more than one individual, and when at least one of them points out the way he or she feels.

24 FRIDAY
Moon Age Day 8 Moon Sign Libra

Beware of outside elements that could so easily prevent you from getting an important message across. You can strive and struggle to say the right thing, but the wrong words are apt to come out. Keep a sense of proportion and, if at all possible, laugh at your own slight inadequacy today.

Your Daily Guide to July 2015

25 SATURDAY
Moon Age Day 9   Moon Sign Scorpio

Take advantage of the planetary trends highlighting your competitive spirit. Although you may not be quite as lucky as proved to be the case yesterday, you make up for this fact with a combination of sheer determination and the odd calculated gamble. All in all, you should enjoy today fully.

26 SUNDAY
Moon Age Day 10   Moon Sign Scorpio

If your social life has been making greater than usual demands on your pocket, now is the time to rein in your spending somewhat. This is particularly true if you have a protracted journey planned. You can't have everything and, short of winning the Lottery, you simply have to save some cash.

27 MONDAY
Moon Age Day 11   Moon Sign Sagittarius

This is a day when you would welcome variety, but unfortunately, it is more likely to be a period during which it is vital to ensure that you do the right thing at the correct moment. Balancing needs and wants is not going to be at all easy, but you will be the loser in the end if you don't.

28 TUESDAY
Moon Age Day 12   Moon Sign Sagittarius

There are gains available by keeping on top of the game at work, though your approach is now more considered than will have been the case last week. People find you slightly more studious and certainly willing to listen to an alternative point of view. You are able to achieve much at present, mainly through hard work.

29 WEDNESDAY
Moon Age Day 13   Moon Sign Capricorn

If you wear a smile all day, life works out that much better for you. The fact is that there is now plenty to smile about, if only because life appears so funny. Taking anything seriously is difficult and you even enjoy those jokes that are pointed in your direction. New friends are probably about to come into your life.

30 THURSDAY
Moon Age Day 14   Moon Sign Capricorn

Any nagging doubts about the direction your life has been taking ought to be fully dispelled now. You are totally in command and should be more than happy with your progress at work, and possibly also in terms of romance. You won't want to take on too much in the way of new responsibility, at least for today.

Your Daily Guide to July 2015

31 FRIDAY
Moon Age Day 15 Moon Sign Aquarius

This is probably going to be a quiet day, but it can also be quite enjoyable. Not everyone you know is being equally kind, though you are inclined to make excuses for one or two of them at present. Create a more comfortable space for yourself as the warmest weather approaches, perhaps in the garden.

2015

Your Month at a Glance

+ = Opportunities are around   − = Be on the defensive   = Life is pretty ordinary

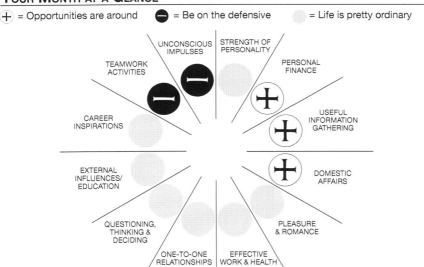

August Highs and Lows

Here I show you how the rhythms of the Moon will affect you this month. Like the tide, your energies and abilities will rise and fall with its pattern. When it is above the centre line, go for it, when it is below, you should be resting.

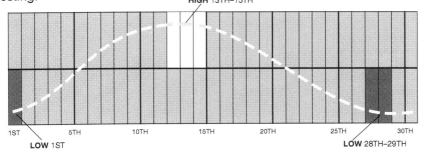

Your Daily Guide to August 2015

1 SATURDAY
Moon Age Day 16   Moon Sign Aquarius

Attend to little jobs today and don't try to push yourself too hard. You are quite creative at the moment and will still want to beautify your surroundings. The slightly odd behaviour of others is something you have to cope with, even if it is more likely to make you laugh than to be annoyed.

2 SUNDAY
Moon Age Day 17   Moon Sign Pisces

A few of your plans might be thrown into chaos, but only for a few hours. The receding lunar low can leave a feeling that you are not really in charge, but it is one you must dispel as quickly as possible. Routines help, plus the realisation that there is assistance around if you need it.

3 MONDAY
Moon Age Day 18   Moon Sign Pisces

Although you are going to great lengths to please others today, in a significant number of cases this could be a waste of energy. It will seem as though some people are quite unwilling to co-operate, no matter how much effort you put in. Don't be annoyed; simply switch your efforts into worthwhile directions instead.

4 TUESDAY
Moon Age Day 19   Moon Sign Aries

The green light is still on, at least in the early part of the day. Later, you could find less support for your schemes and you may discover that not everyone you expected to be on your team wants to play ball. Turn your attention in the direction of love, because your popularity is still high in this sphere of life, and remains so for a while.

5 WEDNESDAY
Moon Age Day 20   Moon Sign Aries

There is the potential for a boost to your ego to lead you to realise how impressive your personality can be when seen through the eyes of others. The need to stand out in a crowd is much emphasised at this time, with the result that your social instincts are stronger than ever. Popularity appears to be yours for the taking.

6 THURSDAY
Moon Age Day 21   Moon Sign Aries

You might be feeling good about family matters today, and concerning something from the past that is replaying itself positively in your life at the moment. Although there are few hours in which you can simply have fun, the practical side of life appeals to you and may prove to be reward enough in itself.

Your Daily Guide to August 2015

7 FRIDAY
Moon Age Day 22   Moon Sign Taurus

Prepare to make the most of a very optimistic frame of mind and milk the situation for all you are worth. There could be financial gains to be made at the end of this working week and great headway in career matters. Don't be too pushy in social settings and allow situations to mature in their own good time.

8 SATURDAY
Moon Age Day 23   Moon Sign Taurus

This is a good time for romance and a weekend that offers a number of wonderful incentives. Avoid being anxious about issues that really do not matter and concentrate on having fun. A long walk might be enjoyable, or alternatively, if the more materialistic side of your nature is on display, a protracted visit to the shops.

9 SUNDAY
Moon Age Day 24   Moon Sign Gemini

Practical duties might turn out to be something of a bind today. If this turns out to be the case, leave them alone. This is Sunday, after all. Spend some time daydreaming and thinking up new ideas that will be useful once another working week begins. At the same time, be prepared to up the pressure in terms of your social life.

10 MONDAY
Moon Age Day 25   Moon Sign Gemini

A sense of personal security might have you looking around your home and wondering how you can better protect what you have. That's fine, just as long as you do not become paranoid about the situation. Stay away from practical new starts, not because of the possibility of failure, but to spend more time with those you love.

11 TUESDAY
Moon Age Day 26   Moon Sign Cancer

There is room to pile most of your energy into your work, and even if you are still studying or perhaps retired, you won't find it hard to fill your hours. Much of what you do is on behalf of others and almost all your tasks today will carry a special sort of satisfaction. Don't be surprised if people are saying nice things about you.

12 WEDNESDAY
Moon Age Day 27   Moon Sign Cancer

Your social and love life should be supplying some light relief now. This is another one of those periods of this summer during which you could be thinking about a trip of some sort, perhaps even a holiday. Present planetary positions might indicate that you are rather quieter than has been the case recently.

Your Daily Guide to August 2015

13 THURSDAY
Moon Age Day 28 Moon Sign Leo

The green light is on now for action and any slight disappointments that attended your working life recently are disappearing fast. Make the most of what today offers in terms of dynamism and determination. Few could resist your overwhelming conviction and positive powers of persuasion now.

14 FRIDAY
Moon Age Day 29 Moon Sign Leo

Take advantage of the lunar high and the planetary trends that are going your way. In a holistic sense, this could turn out to be the very best day of the month. New ideas come into your mind all the time and your intuition is also particularly strong. You can afford to act on impulse.

15 SATURDAY
Moon Age Day 0 Moon Sign Leo

At a practical level, it is clear that certain situations need thinking through very carefully indeed. Don't be too quick to make up your mind about anything, especially if there is a financial angle. You need to feel free at the moment and so will be doing all you can to lift restraints from your life.

16 SUNDAY
Moon Age Day 1 Moon Sign Virgo

Domestic relationships generally look quite good, and, since it's Sunday, you might choose to spend it in the company of family members or maybe even very close friends. Strangers are less likely to figure in your life for the moment and you might even restrict your movement more than has been the case recently.

17 MONDAY
Moon Age Day 2 Moon Sign Virgo

Changes are now inevitable, so if there are aspects of your professional life that have not been working all that well, this would be a good time to revitalise them. You might be surprised by the way specific people are treating you, probably because they are developing a new respect for your abilities.

18 TUESDAY
Moon Age Day 3 Moon Sign Libra

Once again, you find yourself on the move and anxious to make the most of every moment during which you can put forward newer and more dynamic strategies. The spotlight is on romance and you might want to start by thinking up some compliments that nobody could ignore.

Your Daily Guide to August 2015

19 WEDNESDAY
Moon Age Day 4 Moon Sign Libra

There could be unexpected changes in the offing, probably as a result of things you did some time ago. This is a favourable time for a degree of nostalgia; you can replay certain experiences, but this time to get them absolutely right. A special friend is likely to seek you out soon.

20 THURSDAY
Moon Age Day 5 Moon Sign Libra

Your ability to attract just the right sort of person stands you in good stead at the moment. Avoid listening too much to gossip and rumours, sticking only to the sort of facts that you can check out in person. Money matters should be steady, but this is not the time for reckless gambles.

21 FRIDAY
Moon Age Day 6 Moon Sign Scorpio

Although this day is less satisfying in terms of overall success, there is still scope for you to get what you want in less obvious ways. Some people might call your present behaviour a little sneaky, but that is probably because they didn't think up your strategy first. It is possible to score successes, though by using psychology rather than force.

22 SATURDAY
Moon Age Day 7 Moon Sign Scorpio

You will have to keep a closer eye on your budget now, because you are inclined to squander money at the very time you need it the most. An investment in travel could pay handsome dividends, if only in terms of pleasure. With the weekend here, you may decide the time is right to change location.

23 SUNDAY
Moon Age Day 8 Moon Sign Sagittarius

This would be an ideal time to begin new projects, if only because you are unfettered by the sort of details that sometimes get in the way. You should also discover that your general good luck is better, with opportunities to make a few pounds through some fairly safe form of speculation.

24 MONDAY
Moon Age Day 9 Moon Sign Sagittarius

Work matters should proceed very much as expected at this time, even if you have to make some alterations to your plans. Friendship is important now and you tend to support the underdog in just about any situation. What Leo is showing in abundance at present is a great deal of compassion.

Your Daily Guide to August 2015

25 TUESDAY
Moon Age Day 10   Moon Sign Sagittarius

When it comes to working hard and earning money, you are second to none at this time. However, this does not mean you have to spend every second thinking about such matters. On the contrary, this should also be a time when you can leave these issues firmly on the shelf. Concentrate on having some fun.

26 WEDNESDAY
Moon Age Day 11   Moon Sign Capricorn

In personal relationships, you have your work cut out today. It is possible that your partner is behaving in a less than typical manner, whilst you do not show quite the level of patience that would normally be the case. Make a special effort to show that you care, and that your heart is in the right place.

27 THURSDAY
Moon Age Day 12   Moon Sign Capricorn

This ought to be a stable and productive day, particularly in your personal life. It is now much easier to show the people you love that you are sincere and working towards their best interests. Insincerity is not part of your agenda, and there is much to be said for proving this.

28 FRIDAY
Moon Age Day 13   Moon Sign Aquarius

Instant success will not be coming your way today. The lunar low holds back situations and makes it rather difficult for you to make the sort of progress you might wish. Use this as a contemplative period and a time when it is better to look ahead and plan, rather than to push forwards.

29 SATURDAY
Moon Age Day 14   Moon Sign Aquarius

A degree of assistance never goes amiss, and this is what you can expect if you are a Leo who works on a Saturday. The same is generally true in non-professional situations, though in this case you are in a better position to help yourself. Get unsavoury jobs out of the way as early in the day as you can.

30 SUNDAY
Moon Age Day 15   Moon Sign Pisces

Take advantage of the planetary trends that suggest problem-solving could be fun and quite successful today. You now have the ability to go to the heart of any matter and to deal with details in a flash. On a more personal footing, you will be out to prove just how deep and enduring your love actually is.

Your Daily Guide to August 2015

31 MONDAY
Moon Age Day 16 Moon Sign Pisces

Look out for pitfalls in the monetary area of life and avoid too much speculation or outright gambling for the moment. Once again, you could find yourself to be rather too outspoken for your own good and you should avoid reacting to the comments of others, even if you consider them to be outrageous.

September 2015

Your Month at a Glance

(+) = Opportunities are around   (−) = Be on the defensive   ○ = Life is pretty ordinary

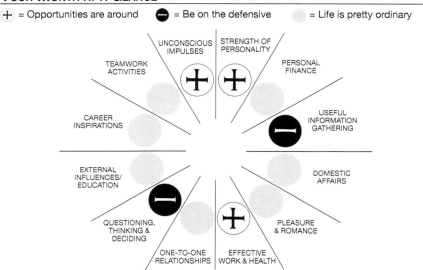

September Highs and Lows

Here I show you how the rhythms of the Moon will affect you this month. Like the tide, your energies and abilities will rise and fall with its pattern. When it is above the centre line, go for it, when it is below, you should be resting.

HIGH 10TH–11TH

LOW 24TH–25TH

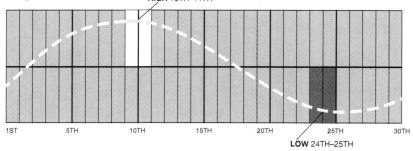

Your Daily Guide to September 2015

1 TUESDAY
Moon Age Day 17 Moon Sign Aries

There is a warning around today that simple oversights on your part could lead to a few mistakes. That is why it is necessary to work slowly and steadily towards your objectives, without rushing or pushing. There is assistance around if you are willing to look for it, though being a Leo subject you probably won't.

2 WEDNESDAY
Moon Age Day 18 Moon Sign Aries

Your mind is inclined to turn towards work and practical matters now. Routines can be rather boring because you want to break down fences and move forwards all the time. This isn't always possible, so for now consolidate your position and try to be patient.

3 THURSDAY
Moon Age Day 19 Moon Sign Taurus

A little extra charm coming from your direction could go a long way in relationships this Friday. Not only can you make others happy, but you are also able to feather your own nest on the way. A partnership of some sort is getting stronger and results come in regarding efforts you have put in recently.

4 FRIDAY
Moon Age Day 20 Moon Sign Taurus

Don't be surprised if you find circumstances conspiring to allow you a greater degree of personal freedom and choice. Grab the moment with both hands and make the most of it. Even a very slight amount of pressure could convince others that your point of view is both measured and sensible today.

5 SATURDAY
Moon Age Day 21 Moon Sign Gemini

You should now be well on top of necessary jobs and may even be quite willing to take a day off. Not that this means you will be idle. On the contrary, you could be in the market for a shopping spree, or for some even more robust sort of activity. Whatever you decide to do, make sure you are supporting other people, too.

6 SUNDAY
Moon Age Day 22 Moon Sign Gemini

Although you could find yourself feeling rather restless at the moment, you can overcome this with a little imagination. Enrol friends in some of your latest enterprises, get out and about when you are not at work, and do your best to cheer everyone up. That should give you plenty to do.

Your Daily Guide to September 2015

7 MONDAY
Moon Age Day 23 Moon Sign Cancer

There is assistance coming from above today. No, you don't need to look to angelic help from some passing cloud, because it is bosses at work or people in positions of influence who could offer you their support. Try not to get too involved in the arguments or discussions of other people. They can only cloud your horizons now.

8 TUESDAY
Moon Age Day 24 Moon Sign Cancer

A wonderfully romantic interlude is on the way. Those Leo subjects who are not directly looking for love could find they are on the receiving end of affection in any case. Try not to do more than you have to early in the day, but by the time the late afternoon and evening come along you are raring to get up and go.

9 WEDNESDAY
Moon Age Day 25 Moon Sign Cancer

Under prevailing circumstances, the peace and quiet you may desire at home today probably won't be forthcoming. People want to visit you and may bring other friends with them. All in all, it could turn out to be an active sort of day. On the one hand you might moan about the fact, but being a Leo subject you should be pleased that life is eventful.

10 THURSDAY
Moon Age Day 26 Moon Sign Leo

Fresh starts are on the way and the lunar high offers you the best incentive this month to pitch in and have a go. This would be a great day for travel, or for putting across to other people some of your most treasured ideas. Confrontation is not necessary, and in any case your razor-sharp wit will deflect it.

11 FRIDAY
Moon Age Day 27 Moon Sign Leo

A physical and mental peak arrives for many sons and daughters of the Sun. Keep up the pressure and let people know what you want from life. There are many occasions today when even strangers would lend a hand if they only knew what it was you are after. Finances should strengthen, as you are spending wisely at present.

12 SATURDAY
Moon Age Day 28 Moon Sign Virgo

You could find you are heading for a more hectic time socially, possibly because of the arrival of the weekend. You haven't really put your feet up for some time and today is like to be no exception to the busy rule. Avoid too much fussing over issues that will sort themselves out if you only give them time.

Your Daily Guide to September 2015

13 SUNDAY
Moon Age Day 0   Moon Sign Virgo

Romantic matters seem to be positively highlighted at this time. If the weather is good, this would be an ideal time to take your lover on a little trip somewhere. It is probably in the evening that the most intimate contacts are available, with a busier daytime period.

14 MONDAY
Moon Age Day 1   Moon Sign Virgo

Don't risk overturning recent successes by being impatient or expecting too much of yourself. A slow and steady sort of Monday is on offer, which turns out to be no bad thing. Socialise when you can and turn your mind once again to showing your loved ones how important they are to you. Emotions are close to the surface.

15 TUESDAY
Moon Age Day 2   Moon Sign Libra

Certain projects demand your attention and it is true that you will want to get them done and finished. All the same you may not be too successful if you rush. It is far better to get a job done properly first time, rather than having to return to it at some future date. Slow and steady wins the race for Leo now.

16 WEDNESDAY
Moon Age Day 3   Moon Sign Libra

You find plenty to do today, especially at work. Even if you are between jobs or retired, you will still keep yourself very busy today. Not everyone appears to have your best interests at heart at the moment, but it is easy for you to spot people who are trying to fool you in some way.

17 THURSDAY
Moon Age Day 4   Moon Sign Scorpio

Beware of unaccountable setbacks to be dealt with today, but in the main you will take these in your stride. Life is fairly competitive, but a Leo will not shy away from this. Even so, the pressure this brings could tire you more quickly than normal. What you need for the end of the day is some sort of alternative.

18 FRIDAY   ☿
Moon Age Day 5   Moon Sign Scorpio

Work matters continue to be very productive and you have little trouble getting your own way. Look ahead, into the distant future, and make some provision now for that time. On the social front, you revel in the company of inspirational people, some of whom have a very special message to impart to you now.

Your Daily Guide to September 2015

19 SATURDAY ☿ *Moon Age Day 6 Moon Sign Scorpio*

There's nothing wrong with seeking out people who you might consider to be either famous, or at least worthy of your adoration. You might enjoy a little notoriety yourself right now, and certainly will not shy away from the chance to shine in any social setting. Keep an eye on money matters.

20 SUNDAY ☿ *Moon Age Day 7 Moon Sign Sagittarius*

There is a chance that there will be a few ups and downs at home right now. You tend to take these in your stride, but if things really get out of hand, the worst case scenario is that you will actively choose to spend social hours with friends, rather than relatives. People in the wider world are very giving at present.

21 MONDAY ☿ *Moon Age Day 8 Moon Sign Sagittarius*

It's not worth taking anything for granted today. Check and recheck facts, especially where travel plans are concerned. If you feel restless at the moment, it is important to ring the changes. Maybe a total change of scene would do you good, preferably in the company of your partner.

22 TUESDAY ☿ *Moon Age Day 9 Moon Sign Capricorn*

Trends alter as the Sun enters your solar third house. Where there have been slight problems in relationships during the last few days, you have the potential now to rediscover your powers of communication. Talk things through rationally and you are likely to have a positive outcome.

23 WEDNESDAY ☿ *Moon Age Day 10 Moon Sign Capricorn*

All matters of communication are now in the spotlight. This is the time of year that you can talk to anyone about almost anything. Trust your own judgement and don't feel that you have to go to great lengths to qualify any belief that seems natural. Your intuition and common sense exist now in equal proportion.

24 THURSDAY ☿ *Moon Age Day 11 Moon Sign Aquarius*

Your powers of vitality are taking something of a dive today. Because you have been galloping along so fast, the sudden brake applied by the lunar low is that much more noticeable. Don't be disheartened. Simply sit back and mull things over for a day or two. Everyone needs a rest, even irrepressible Leo.

Your Daily Guide to September 2015

25 FRIDAY ☿ *Moon Age Day 12   Moon Sign Aquarius*

It might be sensible to put at least a few of your ideas on hold. Instead of dealing with the practicalities of life, spend some time with people you find interesting, and who have a positive view of you. Your ego needs massaging and what you definitely don't require at the moment are comments that belittle you in any way.

26 SATURDAY ☿ *Moon Age Day 13   Moon Sign Pisces*

You won't get everything you want this Saturday, but a great deal depends on your initial expectations. If you are modest in your assessment of possibilities, you can still take pleasure in the day. Stay away from major decisions and opt instead for a strongly social day, with lots of interaction.

27 SUNDAY ☿ *Moon Age Day 14   Moon Sign Pisces*

There are matters in life today that you cannot take for granted, or problems will dog your footsteps. Look carefully at your actions and think carefully before you make any moves. Avoid rash decisions and, if possible, qualify your own thoughts by running them past people you consider to be wise.

28 MONDAY ☿ *Moon Age Day 15   Moon Sign Aries*

Beware of being sidetracked by trivia today. There is so much red tape around that you need mentally to carry a pair of scissors with you. All the more reason to try to see through to the heart of situations and then to act accordingly. Don't be put off by people who seek to confuse you.

29 TUESDAY ☿ *Moon Age Day 16   Moon Sign Aries*

There are some potential high spots in romance today, which many Leo people will not want to miss. Although you are busy planning strategies, you need to take time out to have fun, or else all the effort is a waste of time. Getting ahead professionally is a means to an end, and not an end in itself.

30 WEDNESDAY ☿ *Moon Age Day 17   Moon Sign Taurus*

New initiatives could be on the way in the romantic department of your life. Perhaps you are looking at an existing relationship in a different light, or finding a new love. Family pressures are somewhat reduced now and you make most decisions intuitively today.

2015

Your Month at a Glance

⊕ = Opportunities are around   ⊖ = Be on the defensive   ● = Life is pretty ordinary

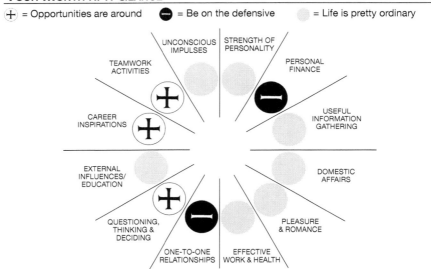

October Highs and Lows

Here I show you how the rhythms of the Moon will affect you this month. Like the tide, your energies and abilities will rise and fall with its pattern. When it is above the centre line, go for it, when it is below, you should be resting.

HIGH 7TH–8TH
LOW 22ND–23RD

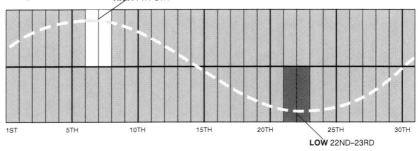

Your Daily Guide to October 2015

1 THURSDAY ☿   *Moon Age Day 18 Moon Sign Taurus*

Prepare to make the most of an intellectual peak at the beginning of October by being in the right place at the best time. Your persuasive talents can be put to the test in a number of different ways: professional, practical and even personal. The fact is that you could sell refrigerators to the Inuit at present.

2 FRIDAY ☿   *Moon Age Day 19 Moon Sign Gemini*

Be prepared for minor tensions, particularly at home. You may decide it is better to spend more time with friends right now, taking the heat off domestic situations. At work you should be active and genuinely taking a role when it proves to be most important to do so.

3 SATURDAY ☿   *Moon Age Day 20 Moon Sign Gemini*

Take advantage of the planetary trends that are highlighting creativity. If you are thinking about making changes in and around your home, it might be a good idea to consult your partner. Other family members also have their part to play and it really is a case of being open to opinion now.

4 SUNDAY ☿   *Moon Age Day 21 Moon Sign Gemini*

You are your own best public relations officer today: frank, fearless and bold, yet at the same time caring and willing to listen. These really are the very best qualities of your zodiac sign and they are available for all to see. As a result you ought to find yourself on the receiving end of a very happy day.

5 MONDAY ☿   *Moon Age Day 22 Moon Sign Cancer*

There is a chance that the information you receive from other people will turn out to be interesting and potentially helpful. For this reason alone it is worth keeping your ears open. Even gossip does not fall beneath your contempt for once, though of course being a Leo subject you certainly won't believe everything you hear.

6 TUESDAY ☿   *Moon Age Day 23 Moon Sign Cancer*

For the first part of the day you will be taking things steadily, but once you get the bit between your teeth, it's onwards and upwards once more. Keep an open mind about the attitudes and opinions of a friend, which may sound radical and even quite bonkers. They may simply be going through a tricky period.

Your Daily Guide to October 2015

7 WEDNESDAY ☿ *Moon Age Day 24 Moon Sign Leo*

You can think big today and tend to make the world your oyster by the sheer dynamism of your personality. Almost anyone you meet can be good to know and useful to have around in a practical sense. What really sets the day apart is the fact that you should be smiling nearly all the time.

8 THURSDAY ☿ *Moon Age Day 25 Moon Sign Leo*

This would be a superb time for putting new ideas into practice. Don't be held back by negative types. Once you have made up your mind, keep moving in that direction. Your social life should be a breeze and with more and more popularity coming your way there are new people joining the fan club.

9 FRIDAY ☿ *Moon Age Day 26 Moon Sign Virgo*

Don't make life any more difficult than it needs to be by chasing up every detail or insisting on having your say. There are times right now when it would definitely be best to keep quiet, rather than to cause problems for yourself. The end of the working week could easily be marred with disputes, though you can avoid them.

10 SATURDAY ☿ *Moon Age Day 27 Moon Sign Virgo*

With the weekend comes a chance to enlist the help and co-operation of other people. It was inevitable right this early in the October that you would vacillate between listening and acting on impulse, but today finds you very compliant. Saturday ought to offer good social prospects and a chance for new enterprises.

11 SUNDAY ☿ *Moon Age Day 28 Moon Sign Virgo*

New and enlivening experiences are just around the next corner. You may become a little frustrated that they don't turn up immediately, but that's the nature of Leo. If you can stay cool, calm and collected, even when you are provoked, there is a good chance you will overcome any obstacle.

12 MONDAY *Moon Age Day 29 Moon Sign Libra*

The spotlight is on your social life, where there could be plenty of lighthearted and enjoyable moments today. Look out for new people coming into your life. They might not signify too much at the moment, but it is only a matter of time before these same individuals begin to play a much more important part in your plans for the future.

Your Daily Guide to October 2015

13 TUESDAY
Moon Age Day 0 Moon Sign Libra

You are well in the groove early in the day, even if a few frustrations come along like little dark clouds to spoil your horizons somewhat later. Life is still quite intense, but there is nothing preventing you from taking a break of some sort. Even a slight change in emphasis would be better than nothing.

14 WEDNESDAY
Moon Age Day 1 Moon Sign Scorpio

Wednesday brings relief from something that has been nagging at you for a while. Circumstances may force you down slower paths, but a little circumspection won't do you any harm at all. Look ahead towards the weekend and work now towards special social functions that have been planned for a while.

15 THURSDAY
Moon Age Day 2 Moon Sign Scorpio

Relationships tend to be rewarding today, which is why you may decide to drop most responsibilities and practical issues in favour of having fun. There are people around who make you laugh, and who are just as fond of you as you are of them. This is definitely not a day during which you need to complicate anything.

16 FRIDAY
Moon Age Day 3 Moon Sign Scorpio

Your co-operative spirit is strong, so don't be afraid to combine your own powers with those of the people you like the most. If there are any individuals around at present who do not care for you, simply shrug your shoulders and accept the fact that you cannot be universally popular.

17 SATURDAY
Moon Age Day 4 Moon Sign Sagittarius

Be prepared for a loved one to rely heavily on your judgement. This implies a high degree of responsibility, but that is not an issue for the Leo nature. You will give the advice you know to be sensible and can be relied upon to offer good counsel and a great deal of natural empathy.

18 SUNDAY
Moon Age Day 5 Moon Sign Sagittarius

You could be in a position to benefit from some good decision-making where money is concerned. Not everyone is willing to support you, however, and you could have trouble with certain acquaintances. In terms of plain friendship, you will find the people who have been around the longest are the ones you want to rely on.

Your Daily Guide to October 2015

19 MONDAY
Moon Age Day 6 Moon Sign Capricorn

When it comes to talking to colleagues today, you stand a chance of getting a very sympathetic ear and even offers of practical assistance. There is a chance for people you haven't seen for ages to come back into your life any time now, and they may bring with them some heartening and even amusing news.

20 TUESDAY
Moon Age Day 7 Moon Sign Capricorn

Remain open to new input and don't close your mind to anything just because it sounds odd at first. You need to stretch credibility now and to show those around you how keen you are to get on in life. It appears that someone quite important has been watching you, and they are likely to let you know it before long.

21 WEDNESDAY
Moon Age Day 8 Moon Sign Capricorn

There may be a few unexpected demands being made of you now, and that means having to be rather more flexible than has been the case during the last few days. This is particularly true in the case of relatives or friends who are having problems. If you are missing someone, get in touch by letter or email.

22 THURSDAY
Moon Age Day 9 Moon Sign Aquarius

The lunar low can drag you down somewhat if you allow it, so you may feel the need to indulge yourself in some way today. The secret is not to swim against the tide, but to wait for better opportunities to come along. In the meantime, cosset yourself.

23 FRIDAY
Moon Age Day 10 Moon Sign Aquarius

Even if you managed to get at least half way through the lunar low without realising it, there is little assistance about for your plans today. It would be best to keep a low profile for the moment, allowing other people to take some of the strain and being willing to accept intervention and advice.

24 SATURDAY
Moon Age Day 11 Moon Sign Pisces

The focus today appears to be on personal relationships. With everything to play for in the emotional stakes and the weekend offering a good deal of incentive, you need to show those around you, and particularly your romantic partner, how much they mean to you. Social highlights abound.

Your Daily Guide to October 2015

25 SUNDAY
Moon Age Day 12 Moon Sign Pisces

It could be that you are putting your point of view across in a way that others would see as being contentious. Be careful that you do not cause offence, even unintentionally. Trying to be tactful all the time won't be easy, but it can pay quite definite dividends, both personally and perhaps even financially.

26 MONDAY
Moon Age Day 13 Moon Sign Aries

Professional issues can be complicated today and need careful handling. However, don't allow them to spill over into your personal and social life, which also demand more of your time at present. Consider the needs of friends today and involve them in your plans, particularly someone who is down in the dumps.

27 TUESDAY
Moon Age Day 14 Moon Sign Aries

Look out for minor conflict with others, particularly in group situations. The fact is that you often want to be top dog. Even when you don't, others think that you belong at the head of things. Resolving such difficulties will take patience and tact – though you will still end up running the show.

28 WEDNESDAY
Moon Age Day 15 Moon Sign Taurus

Financial affairs are favoured today. There could be ways and means to increase your income, but you have to dig hard within your own reserves to put some of them into practice. You won't be tardy when it comes to putting your ideas across, especially when you are in the company of people who already think you well on the way to being a genius.

29 THURSDAY
Moon Age Day 16 Moon Sign Taurus

Certain communication issues can be marred by disagreements, which is a pity at a time when you are getting on famously with almost everyone. Convincing colleagues that your ideas are better than theirs won't be easy, but is necessary all the same. By the evening, you will simply want to have a good time.

30 FRIDAY
Moon Age Day 17 Moon Sign Gemini

There are some issues that seem to be a real chore today, and the sadness is that there is no getting away from them. Better by far to pitch in early and to get such jobs out of the way. Later on, you can begin to have some real fun, doing things that have a constant and lasting appeal.

Your Daily Guide to October 2015

31 SATURDAY
Moon Age Day 18   Moon Sign Gemini

It is unlikely that your home life could be called boring at present. People demand your time and your advice and there is likely to be lots of coming and going. Things could be somewhat quieter if you have to work, however, and you may feel that a little extra incentive is required before long.

November 2015

Your Month at a Glance

(+) = Opportunities are around   (−) = Be on the defensive   ○ = Life is pretty ordinary

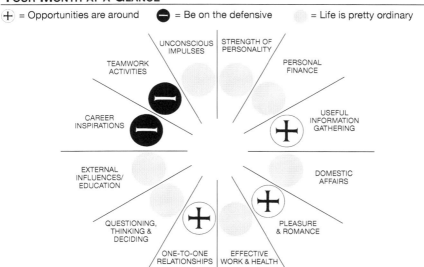

November Highs and Lows

Here I show you how the rhythms of the Moon will affect you this month. Like the tide, your energies and abilities will rise and fall with its pattern. When it is above the centre line, go for it, when it is below, you should be resting.

HIGH 3RD–5TH

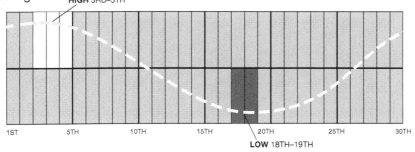

LOW 18TH–19TH

Your Daily Guide to November 2015

1 SUNDAY
Moon Age Day 19   Moon Sign Cancer

A new month, but it's business as usual as far as you are concerned. With plenty to keep you occupied, you look forward positively. What might not appeal to you too much is the approach of winter, but you have the chance to create a warm atmosphere in the next couple of months, no matter what the weather is doing.

2 MONDAY
Moon Age Day 20   Moon Sign Cancer

Your ego is boosted when you are at the forefront of situations, so you won't take kindly to being put at the back of any queue right now. Try to stay calm, even if you feel you are under personal pressure and certainly do not defend yourself when it is obvious to almost everyone that you are not under attack.

3 TUESDAY
Moon Age Day 21   Moon Sign Leo

Press ahead with all major plans and don't allow yourself to be held back when you can see that the going is good. There ought to be plenty to occupy your mind and your body today, with this part of the working week likely to be bringing forth new possibilities of both a professional and a personal nature.

4 WEDNESDAY
Moon Age Day 22   Moon Sign Leo

This would be a good time to put your luck to the test. Although you won't want to put your shirt on the next horse running, there could be gains to be made if you take calculated financial risks. Physically and mentally, most Leo subjects should now be firing on all cylinders.

5 THURSDAY
Moon Age Day 23   Moon Sign Leo

Social and romantic issues ought to prove quite satisfying, probably making for an interesting and even a special sort of period. Personal contentment is present and compared with earlier in the week; you are now less likely to react quickly to issues that are not very important.

6 FRIDAY
Moon Age Day 24   Moon Sign Virgo

Not everything on your agenda can be dealt with as quickly or efficiently as you might wish. This means showing patience and also being willing to allow other people to lend a hand. It might be that you have been holding back specific individuals, simply because you will not relinquish control.

Your Daily Guide to November 2015

7 SATURDAY
Moon Age Day 25   Moon Sign Virgo

There are influences about now that keep you in touch with people you may not see all that often. Your mind tends to travel back as much as it is pushed forwards, and you have a great deal to think about in professional terms. This may turn out to be quite a busy day, though it is diverse and, in most cases, interesting.

8 SUNDAY
Moon Age Day 26   Moon Sign Libra

This might be quite a demanding day, albeit in a low-key sort of way. You move between situations that demand your full attention and there won't be quite the level of rest and relaxation you might wish. There is a forward push on your part to sweep away cobwebs and to see new possibilities that lie before you.

9 MONDAY
Moon Age Day 27   Moon Sign Libra

Your interests are best served by keeping busy and not slacking in any way. People are clearly watching you and the more effort you put in now, the greater the attention focused on you. If you get the chance to take a break later in the day, the change would do you good. Stick with friends at this time.

10 TUESDAY
Moon Age Day 28   Moon Sign Libra

Getting out and about socially may be just what you need to keep a smile on your face today. Too much commitment to practical issues could prove boring and you will feel much happier with some variety in your life. Romantic issues might be on your mind later in the day. Confidence is reasonably high.

11 WEDNESDAY
Moon Age Day 29   Moon Sign Scorpio

This should be a lovely time for all intimate matters. Quite a few planetary indicators are suggesting that love is in the air, together with friendship and a feeling of togetherness. The hard edge of Leo certainly isn't on display at this time and it is likely that certain people will realise what an old softy you really are.

12 THURSDAY
Moon Age Day 0   Moon Sign Scorpio

Be prepared to find yourself suddenly on an emotional roller-coaster. Trying to come to terms with exactly what others expect of you isn't going to be all that easy. Probably the best way to be in the know is the simplest: ask someone!

Your Daily Guide to November 2015

13 FRIDAY
Moon Age Day 1 Moon Sign Sagittarius

Minor disagreements, particularly at home, are really not necessary. Instead of falling out, talk things through calmly and rationally. Friends should be co-operative and anxious to have you with them when the good times roll. Although you might be quite tired today, there is a good chance you will join in.

14 SATURDAY
Moon Age Day 2 Moon Sign Sagittarius

Minor challenges in domestic issues probably cannot be avoided if you stay around at home too much. It would be very easy to become bored during the first part of this weekend. By tomorrow you are on top form again, but for the moment you could do with getting some genuine variety into your life.

15 SUNDAY
Moon Age Day 3 Moon Sign Sagittarius

The emphasis is on creativity today. It could be that you are making changes around house and home, or perhaps getting involved in some new hobby or pastime. Don't spend too much time doing practical things today. There's nothing wrong with having some fun, too.

16 MONDAY
Moon Age Day 4 Moon Sign Capricorn

The value of self-reliance and independence is evident for the sign of the Lion today. All in all, you are in for a fairly positive time. You can't expect everyone to like you, but at least you have it within your nature now to ignore the people who do not. Getting to your chosen objectives ought to be a piece of cake.

17 TUESDAY
Moon Age Day 5 Moon Sign Capricorn

There are opportunities for pleasurable travel, even though this may not be the best part of the year weather-wise. At any rate, you need a change of scenery. Those Leo people who find it possible to take a winter holiday would certainly enjoy getting away now. Consideration for other people appears to he high.

18 WEDNESDAY
Moon Age Day 6 Moon Sign Aquarius

There are some limitations to be faced today and tomorrow. This is more or less entirely due to the lunar low and there probably isn't very much you can do about the situation. Instead of bemoaning the fact, enjoy some rest and relaxation. There is no barrier to having fun, especially when this is of a low-key form.

Your Daily Guide to November 2015

19 THURSDAY
Moon Age Day 7 Moon Sign Aquarius

There is a warning around today not to take any big risks. Be willing to settle for a peaceful life and allow others to take the strain. You are undergoing sea-changes in thinking at the moment and it is helpful for you to take some moments for reflection. In reality, you should get a good deal more done right now than you expect.

20 FRIDAY
Moon Age Day 8 Moon Sign Pisces

Only you can decide whether or not to believe everything you hear today. Be cautious, however, because at least some of it will be true. Confidence is growing all the time in a professional sense, but you can be too clever for your own good. It is important to check and recheck all facts and figures before proceeding with any specific deal.

21 SATURDAY
Moon Age Day 9 Moon Sign Pisces

Get an early start with all important projects and ideas. The more you get done in the morning, the greater the amount of time you will have to please yourself later. It might be difficult to prevent yourself from doing tasks that rightfully belong in the middle of next week, but that's just the way you are feeling now.

22 SUNDAY
Moon Age Day 10 Moon Sign Aries

The green light is on and you are keen to get on with specific projects. The help you need is surely present, though in the main you are happiest when working alone. Not everyone will have your best interests at heart, though it isn't hard to tell who wants to stab you in the back.

23 MONDAY
Moon Age Day 11 Moon Sign Aries

This is a perfect day to be in the thick of things socially and some of the less than positive associations of yesterday are now dissipating fast. Congratulations may be in order somewhere in your friendship circle and you will want to be the first to offer them. Concentrate when dealing with financial matters.

24 TUESDAY
Moon Age Day 12 Moon Sign Taurus

A more competitive edge shows today, especially when you are involved in discussions of any sort. Confidence is growing to overthrow obstacles that have been around a while, especially at work. You are able to score a genuine coup over someone who hasn't shown much interest in your wellbeing.

Your Daily Guide to November 2015

25 WEDNESDAY
Moon Age Day 13 Moon Sign Taurus

You are popular and attractive at the moment, not that this is anything new for the average Leo. All the same, it shows and you can't avoid realising when someone is giving you the come on. Whether or not you respond depends on your availability, but be careful: this is no time to take emotional chances.

26 THURSDAY
Moon Age Day 14 Moon Sign Gemini

There should be no problems with your ego at present. Your popularity remains intact and, once again, it isn't hard for you to notice when people like you. Naturally inclined to speak the truth at the moment, you are drawn into offering the sort of assistance that you would hardly have expected.

27 FRIDAY
Moon Age Day 15 Moon Sign Gemini

Your powers of attraction are in the ascendant and you would rarely find a better day for appealing to someone you have fancied for a while. If this merely represents a fantasy, there is probably no harm done. Don't be too quick to judge a friend who has acted rashly.

28 SATURDAY
Moon Age Day 16 Moon Sign Cancer

It might be a good idea to keep certain plans on ice, if only for today. Everything you want can be yours, but just not right now. Spend time with your friends and maybe an hour or two on your own, planning for the future. Finances need careful handling and, if possible, hang on to money for the moment.

29 SUNDAY
Moon Age Day 17 Moon Sign Cancer

With the Sun now firmly in your solar fourth house, it is fun to be around people you know and like. Although just as sociable as ever, there is still that small matter of trust, which has been bugging you for a few days. When you are with those you have known for years, this won't be a problem.

30 MONDAY
Moon Age Day 18 Moon Sign Cancer

If a mini-crisis turns up on the domestic scene, stop everything and sort it out immediately. In the main, it is the social aspects of life that you still enjoy the most and you probably will not find yourself tied too much to professional considerations. Find a few moments simply to sit and contemplate life.

December 2015

YOUR MONTH AT A GLANCE

+ = Opportunities are around   − = Be on the defensive   = Life is pretty ordinary

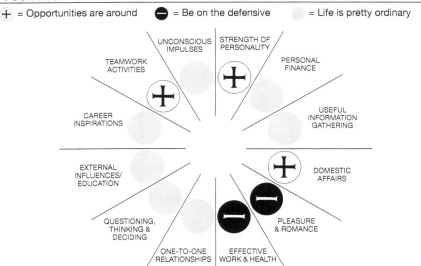

DECEMBER HIGHS AND LOWS

Here I show you how the rhythms of the Moon will affect you this month. Like the tide, your energies and abilities will rise and fall with its pattern. When it is above the centre line, go for it, when it is below, you should be resting.

HIGH 1ST–2ND   HIGH 28TH–29TH

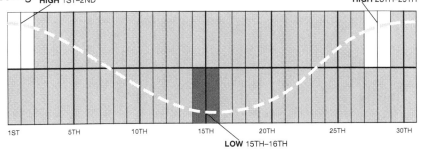

LOW 15TH–16TH

Your Daily Guide to December 2015

1 TUESDAY
Moon Age Day 19 Moon Sign Leo

You could do worse than to stay close to those around you who have real power, particularly at work. Your own ideas are sound, and worth discussing with anyone who is willing to listen. Once work is out of the way, you show a great capacity for simply having a good time.

2 WEDNESDAY
Moon Age Day 20 Moon Sign Leo

This is the best part of the month when it comes to having the necessary get up and go to really change your life and its circumstances. With a good deal of empathy, and a great desire to please others, there is no reason at all why you should ruffle any feathers. Life is hectic, but it should be settled too.

3 THURSDAY
Moon Age Day 21 Moon Sign Virgo

You are aware that give and take is important today and you are unlikely to lose sight of that fact. You might have to be a bit devious if you want to get your own way and yet still let others know how committed you are to them. Don't tell any lies, even if you have to be somewhat liberal with the truth.

4 FRIDAY
Moon Age Day 22 Moon Sign Virgo

Although you could find there are one or two professional setbacks to be addressed, in the main you are still progressive, hopeful and aspirational. Turn your mind away from work later in the day, towards fun and games, which become an increasing part of your life as the month advances. Confidence remains solid.

5 SATURDAY
Moon Age Day 23 Moon Sign Libra

This is a time to be seeking wide, open spaces. The weekend offers a sense of freedom and the chance to do something different. What you wouldn't take kindly to right now is being restricted in any way. There are plenty of people around you who would be only too pleased to join you on a flight of fancy.

6 SUNDAY
Moon Age Day 24 Moon Sign Libra

There are others to contend with today, one or two of whom are anxious for you to follow their lead. To do so probably won't appeal and the difficulty lies in letting them know this fact, without inadvertently offering offence. A little mistake made early in the day should be easy to put right later.

Your Daily Guide to December 2015

7 MONDAY
Moon Age Day 25   Moon Sign Libra

This is a day on which you should have plenty to say for yourself and no shortage of energy with which to get things done. Creature comforts are not all that important to you at the moment and you are quite prepared to go through some discomfort in order to achieve your objectives. You are also extremely friendly today.

8 TUESDAY
Moon Age Day 26   Moon Sign Scorpio

Your best area at the moment comes through travel, mental exercise of almost any sort and simple human contact. Still friendly, and very anxious to help, you seek out good causes right now and do whatever you can to get the rest of the world into the same pre-Christmas spirit that you presently experience.

9 WEDNESDAY
Moon Age Day 27   Moon Sign Scorpio

Your interests are best served by going with the flow today. There are gains to be made in a number of different directions and as you already have your social head on, the run-up to Christmas probably begins here for you. Concentrate on specific tasks that could prove awkward if you lose sight of the major objectives.

10 THURSDAY
Moon Age Day 28   Moon Sign Sagittarius

Look out for small pressures coming from a number of different directions. Calm down an overactive nervous system and avoid allowing yourself to be become too fixated about any aspect of life. Cool and steady is what works for you best this Thursday, and you are more than capable of adopting this state.

11 FRIDAY
Moon Age Day 0   Moon Sign Sagittarius

This could be one of the best days of the month for a new start at work. Of course, you might find this difficult with Christmas just around the corner, but you can start a few balls rolling and will probably be pleased to do so. Co-operation with co-workers can also be a key to success.

12 SATURDAY
Moon Age Day 1   Moon Sign Sagittarius

Since work matters seem to be fairly progressive and, in the main, looking after themselves, you will probably be turning your attention to other matters. Confidence remains generally high on the social scene, and you may decide to embark upon new interests that have been at the back of your mind for a while.

Your Daily Guide to December 2015

13 SUNDAY
Moon Age Day 2   Moon Sign Capricorn

A loved one, perhaps your romantic partner, will probably be expressing some rather strong opinions at present. Be creative in your responses and don't allow yourself to become unsettled by matters that you can deal with quite easily. There are some interesting opportunities to change aspects of your personal life.

14 MONDAY
Moon Age Day 3   Moon Sign Capricorn

Don't be afraid to stand out in a crowd, because your ego requires boosting as much as possible. Avoid family arguments, which cannot help you in any way at the moment, and try to take a generally optimistic view of life. Give yourself chance to relax, once the daily grind is over.

15 TUESDAY
Moon Age Day 4   Moon Sign Aquarius

There is much to be said for avoiding too much work today. The lunar low makes you lethargic and much more willing than usual to put your feet up. Keep a low profile socially, too, maybe settling for spending some hours on your own. The rest should do you good.

16 WEDNESDAY
Moon Age Day 5   Moon Sign Aquarius

This may be another reasonably quiet day. For those Leo subjects who already have their Christmas heads on, this might be a good period to look ahead and to plan. This ought to be a slightly better day on the social front and romance is around for those of you who want to make yourselves available to greet it.

17 THURSDAY
Moon Age Day 6   Moon Sign Pisces

Doing your own thing seems to be the key to happiness at the moment, though maybe you have things slightly wrong. Join in some family fun and you will lighten the professional load you could be carrying at present. There is a need to bolster the resolve of a friend who is trying to alter his or her life. Only you can help with this.

18 FRIDAY
Moon Age Day 7   Moon Sign Pisces

Although your sense of professional commitment is reasonably good, you should be turning your attention towards the practical necessities of life today. Getting ready for Christmas is one thing that you address and you may also be busy working out how to improve general family resources in the weeks ahead.

Your Daily Guide to December 2015

19 SATURDAY
Moon Age Day 8 Moon Sign Aries

High spirits prevail, and the sense of joy that is so important to your zodiac sign is well in evidence. Not everyone is quite as happy as you are today, though you do have the capacity to cheer up others if you put your mind to the task. Personal issues demand a matter of fact attitude at present.

20 SUNDAY
Moon Age Day 9 Moon Sign Aries

There are a number of obligations around today that leave little time for you to concentrate on your own life. Since this is fairly typical of the sort of person you are, it probably will not worry you too much, if at all. Last-minute planning for Christmas is part of the recipe for an interesting Sunday.

21 MONDAY
Moon Age Day 10 Moon Sign Aries

Avoid being too extravagant today. There is a possibility that you are spending money you don't actually possess, and this could lead to a few worries towards the very end of the year or in January. You need to be realistic, and to persuade those around you to take a similar attitude.

22 TUESDAY
Moon Age Day 11 Moon Sign Taurus

What matters most today is feeling useful and being able to offer sound advice to people who have problems of one sort or another. You are entering a very positive phase romantically speaking, and one that predominates until well after Christmas. Not everyone is being equally co-operative, however.

23 WEDNESDAY
Moon Age Day 12 Moon Sign Taurus

Practical matters are likely to turn out the way you would wish. Last-minute planning and preparations should go well, but you could be slightly bothered by the attitude of friends, which seems odd. Family members will be pestering you all the time, especially younger people, but this probably won't be a problem to you.

24 THURSDAY
Moon Age Day 13 Moon Sign Gemini

Prepare to make the most of a brand-new influence that increases your desire for new experiences and causes you to throw over traditions and routines willingly. This is fine for you, but with Christmas only just around the corner, you have to respect the fact that some people close to you want to leave things the way they are.

Your Daily Guide to December 2015

25 FRIDAY
Moon Age Day 14   Moon Sign Gemini

There is something distinctly weird and wonderful about Christmas Day, though not in a difficult sense. Out-of-the-ordinary experiences are likely, together with messages from people you may not have been in contact with for ages. All in all, this is a day for good communications and for enjoying the antics of others.

26 SATURDAY
Moon Age Day 15   Moon Sign Cancer

Boxing Day will find you busy and very progressive in attitude. However, the important aspects of today could easily be romantic ones. Maybe it's the time of year or perhaps your own attitude, but you should find that your partner is very much more responsive and inclined to say just the right things to you.

27 SUNDAY
Moon Age Day 16   Moon Sign Cancer

It is clear that you want to remain busy and useful at this time, though you fall short of the total energy that is coming your way tomorrow. It is no sin to take a rest and after all that is part of what holidays are about. Don't shy away from a discussion that you know to be absolutely necessary.

28 MONDAY
Moon Age Day 17   Moon Sign Leo

The lunar high arrives today, adding extra oomph to your life and putting you in a party mood that might not have been totally present so far this Christmas. It takes people with real energy to keep up with you and you tend to mix best with those who hold similar values to your own.

29 TUESDAY
Moon Age Day 18   Moon Sign Leo

You can learn something new and exciting now. Keep your ears open and be willing to alter your plans at the last minute in order to achieve something splendid. The period between Christmas and New Year is turning out to be a hectic, but don't forget that part of the reason for holidays is to have a rest.

30 WEDNESDAY
Moon Age Day 19   Moon Sign Virgo

You can afford to say exactly what you feel, and yet make everyone around you feel very special indeed. Surprises are in store, which isn't all that odd at this time, though some of them will far surpass your expectations.

31 THURSDAY

 Moon Age Day 20 Moon Sign Virgo

Your social life ought to prove quite rewarding. Creative potential is good and you may have decided to make some sort of change at home. As long as it is something that makes you more comfortable and not less, then your efforts are worthwhile. Let someone else undertake a domestic task.

How to Calculate Your Rising Sign

Most astrologers agree that, next to the Sun Sign, the most important influence on any person is the Rising Sign at the time of their birth. The Rising Sign represents the astrological sign that was rising over the eastern horizon when each and every one of us came into the world. It is sometimes also called the Ascendant.

Let us suppose, for example, that you were born with the Sun in the zodiac sign of Libra. This would bestow certain characteristics on you that are likely to be shared by all other Librans. However, a Libran with Aries Rising would show a very different attitude towards life, and of course relationships, than a Libran with Pisces Rising.

For these reasons, this book shows how your zodiac Rising Sign has a bearing on all the possible positions of the Sun at birth. Simply look through the Aries table opposite.

As long as you know your approximate time of birth the graph will show you how to discover your Rising Sign.

Look across the top of the graph of your zodiac sign to find your date of birth, and down the side for your birth time (I have used Greenwich Mean Time). Where they cross is your Rising Sign. Don't forget to subtract an hour (or two) if appropriate for Summer Time.

Rising Signs for Leo

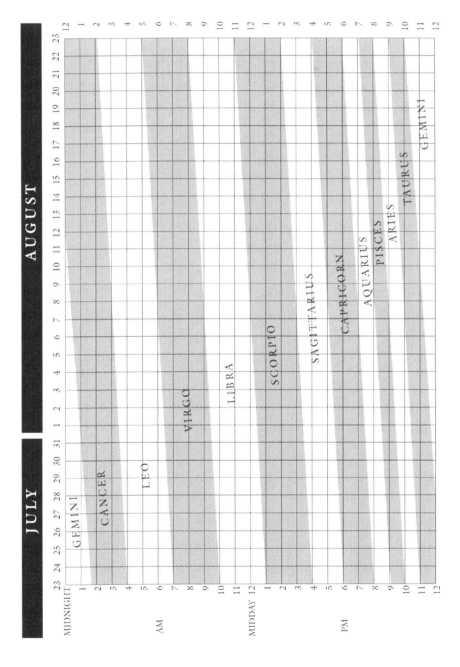

THE ZODIAC, PLANETS AND CORRESPONDENCES

The Earth revolves around the Sun once every calendar year, so when viewed from Earth the Sun appears in a different part of the sky as the year progresses. In astrology, these parts of the sky are divided into the signs of the zodiac and this means that the signs are organised in a circle. The circle begins with Aries and ends with Pisces.

Taking the zodiac sign as a starting point, astrologers then work with all the positions of planets, stars and many other factors to calculate horoscopes and birth charts and tell us what the stars have in store for us.

The table below shows the planets and Elements for each of the signs of the zodiac. Each sign belongs to one of the four Elements: Fire, Air, Earth or Water. Fire signs are creative and enthusiastic; Air signs are mentally active and thoughtful; Earth signs are constructive and practical; Water signs are emotional and have strong feelings.

It also shows the metals and gemstones associated with, or corresponding with, each sign. The correspondence is made when a metal or stone possesses properties that are held in common with a particular sign of the zodiac.

Finally, the table shows the opposite of each star sign – this is the opposite sign in the astrological circle.

Placed	Sign	Symbol	Element	Planet	Metal	Stone	Opposite
1	Aries	Ram	Fire	Mars	Iron	Bloodstone	Libra
2	Taurus	Bull	Earth	Venus	Copper	Sapphire	Scorpio
3	Gemini	Twins	Air	Mercury	Mercury	Tiger's Eye	Sagittarius
4	Cancer	Crab	Water	Moon	Silver	Pearl	Capricorn
5	Leo	Lion	Fire	Sun	Gold	Ruby	Aquarius
6	Virgo	Maiden	Earth	Mercury	Mercury	Sardonyx	Pisces
7	Libra	Scales	Air	Venus	Copper	Sapphire	Aries
8	Scorpio	Scorpion	Water	Pluto	Plutonium	Jasper	Taurus
9	Sagittarius	Archer	Fire	Jupiter	Tin	Topaz	Gemini
10	Capricorn	Goat	Earth	Saturn	Lead	Black Onyx	Cancer
11	Aquarius	Waterbearer	Air	Uranus	Uranium	Amethyst	Leo
12	Pisces	Fishes	Water	Neptune	Tin	Moonstone	Virgo

Printed in Great Britain
by Amazon.co.uk, Ltd.,
Marston Gate.